Eclectic Dust from A Cluttered Mind

A Collection of Short Stories

K. F. Whatley

Published by KF Whatley
Zebulon, North Carolina USA

Eclectic Dust from A Cluttered Mind

A Collection of Short Stories

Copyright © 2021 by K. F. Whatley

All rights reserved. This book or parts thereof may not be reproduced in any form, stored in any retrieval system, or transmitted in any form by any means — electronic, mechanical, photocopy, recording, or otherwise — without prior written permission of the author, except as provided by United States of America copyright law. For permission requests, write to kfw@fictionwriternc.com.

Paperback ISBN: 978-1-7359260-6-3

Cover art by Robin Casey

First Printing 2021 by KF Whatley

www.FictionWriterNC.com

The characters, locations, and actions in this book are fictional. Any resemblance to actual persons living or dead, or supernatural events, is coincidental. Movies, books, lyrics, and other cultural items referenced are copyright their respective owners.

Life is a collection of stories, both real and imagined

Other works by this author

    Making Corrections: A Time Travel Novel
    Triad of Time: A Time Travel Novel *(sequel)*

Acknowledgements

Thank you to my daughter Juli, for not only encouraging me to publish this collection, but arranging for the cover design. Thanks also to my family and friends who read my stories and helped to bring this collection together. To the Second Cup Writers' Group, I appreciate all of your comments and encouragement during our monthly meetings.

Contents

Reanimation Station 1
Suspicious Tech 15
One New Voicemail 19
Long Shadows 25
Miss You 33
Freya's Friend. 35
Taking Notes 39
Beyond the Werewolf. 47
New in Town 53
The Shimmering House 61
The Ashes. 65
A Trick of the Memory 91
Growing Old. 95
After All The Waiting 103
The Camouflaged Woman 107
A Trick of the Light 115
The Corrupted Ones 121
About The Author 131

Reanimation Station

Mr. Morris owned the funeral home. He was a somber but pleasant man, and to Corrie quite different from her previous boss. She wasn't sure what she'd expected — maybe to be working for someone who was more Lurch Addams than normal, kind Mr. Morris. Instead, she'd found the boss and overall environment to be a major improvement over her restaurant job.

It was her first week working at the Morris Mortuary. So far, she'd helped behind-the-scenes with more than a few funerals. The tasks assigned to her were easy, she thought. Before mourners arrived, she vacuumed, placed flowers under the direction of the florist, set out pamphlets, and did pretty much anything for which Mr. Morris and the other workers needed an extra pair of hands.

Body-related tasks were not included in her duties. Mr. Morris' assistants unloaded and rolled in bodies, then loaded them into the hearse for the drive to the cemetery. Everything with the bodies in the between times was done by Mr. Morris himself.

During funerals, he encouraged Corrie to remain in the work rooms and leave the families to him and the more experienced workers. "They know how to be with the grieving families," he'd explained, "and how to keep silent or say carefully measured, appropriate words of comfort." She was too new to do that.

So, Corrie stayed out of sight until Mr. Morris and his main staff left to lead the mourners to the cemetery. Then, Corrie cleaned up and re-vacuumed the first-floor parlor and chapel.

Corrie, who preferred the nickname to her full name, Cordelia, had applied for the job mere days after she and her aging mother moved to Hope Wells, North Carolina. Despite her inexperience, Mr. Morris had hired Corrie immediately after hearing that Corrie's mother worked in a funeral home before they moved to town and her mother retired. In fact, Mr. Morris recognized her mother's name, Amelia Best, which had surprised Corrie. She'd mentioned it to her mother that evening, and the older woman had merely smiled.

Mostly Corrie found the job to be easy, even calming in a way. She enjoyed it more than the restaurant job she'd held for the past ten years. Mr. Morris was good at going with the flow, and he always knew who was arriving, when, and what needed to be done ahead of a dearly-departed's arrival. "I have a plethora of tasks for you," he would say to her each time.

Today she'd been tidying up, helping one of the assistants with a supply order, and picking up food for everyone from the downtown diner. The afternoon was expected to be busy. Two bodies would be arriving, Mr. Morris already had a body-in-waiting, and one "guest" — a 99-year-old man named Sully Becket — ready for a 2PM service.

Mr. Morris always referred to the bodies as *guests*, and everyone else who worked there followed his lead.

One of Corrie's favorite tasks so far was placing flowers in preparation for a viewing or service. The florist, a tightly wound, middle-aged woman, fluttered around the room pointing. Often, she'd direct Corrie to move flower arrangements three or four times before deciding placement was "Absolutely perfect." Corrie didn't mind; she enjoyed being near the flowers and smelling their scents; a passion she'd picked up working in her mother's garden.

After Corrie and two other workers finished with the many flowers for their latest *guest*, the florist scuttled through her good-byes. Corrie heard the van's engine gunning as the florist drove away, heading noisily toward downtown.

Mr. Morris directed two other workers to sweep the "flower droppings" as he called them from the rugs, and he sent Corrie outside to sweep the leaves from the drive and parking area. She grabbed her light jacket and headed out into the crisp fall air with a push broom that looked older than she was; that was saying something as Corrie was thirty. Leaning the ancient broom against the brick building, she whipped a hair tie from her pocket and swirled her long, chestnut hair into a loose pile on top of her head.

Surveying the parking lot, she decided to sweep the leaves from the entrance toward the building's rear corner, where there was a bit of a slope. That would put the leaves out of sight of mourners arriving for the service.

As she began sweeping the front entrance, she drifted into a calm, happy frame of mind with the push broom moving automatically. She enjoyed the hum of easy work like this; it cleared her mind.

By the time the last leaves fluttered down the slope onto the pile, she was sweating. The cool breeze blew over her salty skin, causing a shiver to match with the rustling leaves. She fought back a sudden urge to jump into the leaf pile, giggled, then turned to survey the swept lot. New leaves had fallen since she'd passed, and she frowned at them. Otherwise, she felt the satisfaction of a job well done. Or, at least *done* — until the wind picked up.

Checking the time on her smart phone, she saw that the task had taken an hour. *Not bad for the first time. Next time*, she told herself, *I'll get it done in 50 minutes.*

Pulling a few clinging leaves off the broom, pieces of the brush escaping with them, she leaned the handle against the outside wall and walked inside, stripping off her jacket as the heating assailed her.

She headed for Mr. Morris' work room to ask what task she should do next. Reaching the door and turning the knob, was surprised to find it locked. Knocking lightly on the door, she called, "Sir, it's Corrie. Are you in there?"

No response. She knocked again.

After a moment, she heard a shuffling noise on the other side of the door. Then, faintly, Mr. Morris answered, "Yes, yes. Just a minute."

It felt to Corrie like five or more minutes before her boss finally opened the door. He turned and walked back toward his worktable and Corrie followed. She saw that he was working on a body that had arrived yesterday evening.

"This is Mrs. Castro," he said waving graciously toward the body on the table, as if introducing a friend and not a cold corpse. "So sad. So young."

Corrie looked at the prone woman, guessing that she must have been in her mid-forties — half the age of eighty-nine years old Mr. Morris. "Yes, she is so young," Corrie responded politely. Even at thirty, Corrie didn't feel a kinship with Mrs. Castro, nor close enough to her age for a shiver.

Mr. Morris handed a list to Corrie, "I have a plethora of tasks for you," and he went back to his work, gently smoothing Mrs. Castro's clothing — a task he'll have to do again when she's moved into her casket, Corrie mused.

Nothing on the list was difficult, no one interrupted Corrie's work, and she completed every to-do in a few hours, managing to stay out of sight during the service for Mr. Becket's family and friends.

She had just stowed the bathroom cleaning supplies when Mr. Morris returned from the cemetery in the hearse. She headed for his work room and met him at its door.

"Tomorrow Angela will be in to make Mrs. Castro look pretty." He turned to Corrie. "Would you please check if the family has dropped off a hat for her? Her daughter called earlier and asked if we would put her favorite hat on her."

"I'll go check," Corrie said. She jogged upstairs to the first floor Reception area. Marcus was seated at the desk there, sun streaming through the windows adding highlights to his curly hair. Street noises drifted in through the glass entryway, where the door was propped open. A few errant leaves crossed the floor, and Corrie made a mental note to sweep them.

Marcus didn't look up from his keyboard. Instead, he picked up a paper bag from his desk and held it out toward her. "You want Mrs. Castro's hat, right?"

Corrie took the bag. "Yes, how did you know?"

Marcus still didn't look up, but she saw his lips slip into a Mona Lisa smile. "I've worked here a while," he said.

Corrie returned to the work room with the bag, bouncing down the stairs two at a time. She set the bagged hat on the table where earlier Mrs. Castro's body had lain. Mr. Morris nodded to her, and continued what he'd been doing, which was writing in a ledger he held balanced on the handle of the body storage door.

Corrie checked the time on her smart phone. It was five minutes to quitting time.

As if reading her thoughts, Mr. Morris said, "I'll see you tomorrow, Corrie. Have a good evening." Without looking up, he waved good-bye with his pen hand, then continued writing.

***

That evening as Corrie recounted her day to her mother, Amelia Best clapped. Over the well-seasoned roast her mother prepared, the older woman chattered and shared stories from her own days of working.

After dinner was done, bellies full to bursting, Corrie cleaned the kitchen and headed for bed. Her mother's heavy, flavorful roast always left her feeling tired. As she drifted off to sleep, Corrie wondered if there were other families which spoke wistfully about funerals over dinner.

***

The next day when Corrie arrived at 8AM, Mr. Morris called her into his office. He motioned to a chair and she sat.

"Today, young lady," he paused. "I'm sorry. I know that's not 'politically correct' but I'm old and I forget."

"That's okay."

He continued. "Corrie, I want you to do a few new tasks today. I'd like you to help Angela get Mrs. Castro ready for her viewing. Nothing hands-on, just assist Angela. You watch, though, so you understand what is done for each of our guests."

Corrie nodded.

Corrie watched Angela apply make-up, fix Mrs. Castro's hair, put on her hat, and fuss over her in general. Angela barely spoke, except whispers to Mrs. Castro. A few times, she asked Corrie to hand her a tissue or fetch something from her bag.

When Angela finished, Marcus and one of the part-time workers, Juan, came to move Mrs. Castro into the next room where her casket awaited. After, Mrs. Castro would be moved upstairs, where her family would purr over how beautiful she looked, her wonderful hat, and sweet memories of her life.

***

The longer she worked there, the more Corrie awoke eager to get to the Morris Mortuary for her shift. She cleaned, ordered supplies, organized areas, and learned new things every day. Guest bodies came and went. Services drew conglomerations of grieving relatives in and out. Every day was busy, though following Mr. Morris' lead, the staff worked calmly and with reverence. Corrie became more and more impressed with each day that she worked at Morris Mortuary.

When she'd worked at the restaurant, even as employees changed over the years, people fussed and fretted at each other, occasionally coming to blows in the kitchen, which Corrie believed to be the surly owner's doing. It was wonderful to work in such a professional and pleasant workplace, with a kindhearted man at the helm. Despite the business' focus on death, life flowed joyously through everyone.

Before she knew it, Corrie had worked a full month. She picked up her first paycheck and reveled at the money she'd earned with so little turmoil.

That night, she shared her feelings with her mother, who expressed her happiness that Corrie found the work as satisfying as she had. Mrs. Best spent thirty years working in funeral homes before retiring.

***

Late one Friday evening, Corrie checked the time and was shocked to find that it was more than an hour past quitting time. She couldn't believe it. *Time flies when you're having fun*, she thought, then cringed. This place shouldn't be described as fun; that seemed ghoulish. Still, there was no denying that Mr. Morris ran a tight ship without ruffling feathers.

She grabbed her jacket and walked into Mr. Morris' office. He wasn't there. She turned and walked down the hall to his work room. The door was closed. Grasping the door knob, she turned it and the door clicked. It wasn't locked this time.

Corrie swung the door wide and entered the room, opening her mouth to call to Mr. Morris, and froze. What she saw made her mouth go dry.

"Don't panic," Mr. Morris said. Mr. Morris stood next to his work table, buttoning the suit coat of a man standing in front of him. Corrie couldn't remember the man's name — a guest who had been delivered that afternoon. He, it, was standing. It turned its head to look at her.

Too late, she thought. Corrie's throat tightened as the gears turning in her head ground to a halt.

She screamed.

A hand squeezed her shoulder, and she heard Mr. Morris speaking above the grinding noise in her head. "Calm. Calm. It's all right, Corrie. Everything is all right." His hand squeezed her shoulder again, and she felt his other hand begin to pat her on the back.

She screamed a second time, but it fizzled into a long, drawn out squeak.

"Good. Good," said Mr. Morris. "Good. Calm." He patted her back again and let go of her shoulder.

The guest was still standing next to the worktable. He — it — was staring at her, or maybe at Mr. Morris. With the eyes cloudy, she couldn't tell for sure. She made gurgling noises but didn't scream again.

"Okay, much better. This has been a shock. I should have locked the door," He looked at her questioningly. "I thought you'd gone home already."

"Lost track... track of time," Corrie whispered through her dry mouth. Mr. Morris stood silently. "What's... What's..." but no more words came out.

"Nothing bad. It's nothing bad, child. Give me a moment and I'll explain."

He walked back to where the guest was standing. The guest stopped staring at Corrie and turned its — his — eyes toward Mr. Morris.

"Mr. Palmer, please return to the table for me. It's time for you to rest." Mr. Morris tapped lightly and a metallic *ting* sounded from the table. The guest, Mr. Palmer, stepped upon a stool at the end of the table and pulled himself up. He sat with a thump, and Corrie cringed at the sound. Then, the guest lay flat, Mr. Morris delicately straightening the guest's suit. "Good, sir. Godspeed to you," said Mr. Morris. He reached out and closed Mr. Palmer's eyelids, murmuring words Corrie didn't recognize.

The body, prone on the table, let out a great sigh. It didn't move again.

"There," Mr. Morris said, turning toward Corrie. "Now he is at peace, and you and I need to have a talk." He took her arm and started to lead her out of the room, "We'll go to my office, Corrie."

She realized, as she turned and allowed him to pull her forward, that she'd wet her pants.

For the next fifteen minutes, Mr. Morris talked at Corrie. Corrie sat and listened. She didn't even realize she was in wet clothes anymore. She was horrified and enthralled at the same time, listening to Mr. Morris.

The gist of it was, he explained, that as he had aged, certain tasks became harder to complete alone. One of his part-time workers, Anna, saw him struggling and revealed to him that she dabbled in what she called "benign yet useful energies," having learned to harness them from her mother and grandmother. Anna had introduced Mr. Morris to a form of magic, including an herbal concoction, coupled with spoken phrases, for re-animating the dead. "Not permanently," he explained to Corrie, as if that lessened the horror of it. "Anna's herbs give me a way to bring a guest back with enough energy that it can follow my commands. Guests can dress themselves, and do the heavy lifting for me by getting down from the table, then returning to it once they're clothed. Then, I can put them to rest again."

Corrie believed every word, which she found a little frightening.

"You caught me just at the wrong moment, when Mr. Palmer was assisting me."

"Um," Corrie managed, her mind swirling, overwhelmed with the thought of a body *assisting* with its own preparations for burial. Her stomach flopped, and she folded her hands across her belly.

"Go home, Corrie. We can talk about this another day, or not talk about this at all. We will see how you feel, all right?"

She rose from the chair, nodded at him, then picked up her jacket and walked out. "Good night," she said over her shoulder.

***

A few weeks went by, Corrie working with her head down, and avoiding talking to Mr. Morris about what she'd seen. Her boss didn't broach the subject either.

Then, one evening as Corrie was pushing her dinner around on her plate, her mother asked, "Cordelia, what is bothering you?"

Haltingly, Corrie told her mom, "I saw something disturbing at work last month."

Leaning back in her chair, Amelia raised an eyebrow, staring at her daughter. "You're thirty years old. Don't tell me you're going to start hiding things from me now?"

"I'm not sure what you'll think," Corrie started; then, the whole tale spilled out.

When she'd finished, her face pale, Corrie watched her mother. Amelia's face contorted, and Corrie thought her mom was going to scream. Instead, after a few contortions, she burst out laughing.

"My dear, darling Cordelia. My dear," Amelia said, wiping tears from her now red face. "I'm sorry that it is I who have hidden too much from you."

"What, Mom?" Corrie asked, fearing what was coming.

Amelia stood and leaned over to hug her daughter. "The *Anna* who helped your Mr. Morris is your *auntie* Anna."

Aunt Anna, who rarely visited. Even when she did come by, she practically ignored Corrie, choosing instead to chatter with Amelia to all hours of the night. Corrie's thoughts twisted, then snapped. Aunt Anna worked in a funeral parlor, just as Amelia had.

"You used magic, mom?" Corrie's question came out in a whisper.

"Useful energies, my dear."

***

Corrie awoke the next morning, dizzied by her mother's revelation. As she stood at the kitchen's window watching a few, far between snowflakes fall, Mr. Morris called. He asked if Corrie would come into work early. "I would like you to help me with one of today's guests, he said.

Amelia practically pushed her daughter out the front door. "Go. Go see," her mother said, raising Corrie's suspicions.

***

As soon as Corrie walked into his work room, Mr. Morris handed her a small, cloth sachet of what looked like tea leaves.

"Your mother called me last night. We had a most interesting conversation, and I believe you and she did, too. It was such a pleasure to speak to her, having heard such good things about her all these years. So, today, I'd like you to assist me in waking our guest, so he may dress for his service."

Corrie backed away, stricken. Mr. Morris patted her arm. Soothingly, he said, "You'll understand once you've done it. It's not a bad thing." Chuckling, he pushed her toward the worktable. "It's in your blood. You'll see." He stood beside her, mimicking the spread of herbs by wiggling his fingers in the air over the corpse.

He directed her as she sprinkled a little of the herbal mix, then a little more, and the two stood silently watching the body.

Then, Mr. Morris mumbled a few words she didn't understand. To Corrie, he said, "Sometimes it takes a few minutes, and sometimes a little more of the dried blend."

Mr. Morris nudged her, and she tossed yet another bit of the herbs at the naked corpse, all the while leaning backward to get her upper body as far from it as she could. She'd seen few naked bodies in her life before starting this job, and never one so wrinkly, shriveled, and pale.

At that moment, Marcus stuck his head in and called to Mr. Morris. "We have another arrival, sir. Could you please come and sign for it?" Noticing Corrie, Marcus added, "Good morning, Corrie."

"Oh, yes. I can." Surprise showed on Mr. Morris' face. "I thought I locked the door. Be right with you, Marcus."

Mr. Morris patted Corrie on the back and excused himself, assuring her that he'd be back immediately. Corrie, left on her own, sprinkled more of the tea leaves. Nothing happened. She sprinkled a little more.

Suddenly, the corpse jumped up from the table, its head furtively looking around with vacant, milky eyes. It began shuffling to-and-fro around the room. Horrified, Corrie ducked behind the worktable, watching it, and wishing for her boss' return.

Seconds passed. The corpse circled the work room, Corrie too afraid to touch it. Unguided, it continued rambling into the hall. Marcus and Mr. Morris had left the door ajar!

Corrie followed, realizing that it, he, whatever, was heading toward the stairs that led up to the viewing rooms. She feared that the people who were upstairs for a funeral service might see the odd-looking, dim-eyed man moving around in his full glory, and she rushed to block it.

As it clumped up a step, wavering more than once but not falling, she forced herself forward. She grimaced as she squeezed past the animated body and the stair railing, stifling a retch. Corrie stopped several steps up and held her arms out to block its passage.

Luckily, the walking thing couldn't figure out how to climb a second step. She asked it, "Wouldn't you like to go back to the work room and get on the table?" It lifted a leg and she whimpered, averting her eyes, and crossing her arms across her stomach again.

Mr. Morris appeared at that moment. "Ah," he said, shaking his head. "My apologies. I should have been there for the two of you. It takes experience and patience to not keep adding herbs. It's all right, Corrie."

Mr. Morris commanded the body to return to the work room. Gently, he asked a second time. It turned its head toward the Mortician. Then, Corrie breathed a sigh of relief as the guest thumped from the step to the floor — tilting dangerously for a moment — and began to follow Mr. Morris.

Corrie brought up the rear, slowly, and entered the work room as the body returned to the table. Mr. Morris muttered words, and the guest gave up its energy.

Corrie, reeling from the close call with the corpse-man, discovered that she was covered in sweat.

"Next time, Corrie," Mr. Morris said, mopping sweat from his brow, "use less herbs."

Suspicious Tech

While playing solitaire on her smart phone, Maya's usual way of lulling herself to sleep, an ad popped up in the game. It grabbed her full attention.

Her mind had been drifting; her most recent thought was how her knee hurt from her fall earlier in the day. Now, the advertisement displayed by the game pitched a topical medicine for joint pain, as if it knew what she'd been thinking. She stared at the ad, momentarily puzzled, then dismissed it, and began playing the next game of solitaire.

She knew that game ads were targeted to online activity. Frequently, ads for cat food popped up and she understood it was because she bought their canned food online. But, reviewing her day, she couldn't recall posting about her knee injury. She hadn't searched for medicine either, or mentioned her knee aloud to anyone — not even the cats.

It's just an anomaly. I haven't seen an ad for knee medicine before, but it's got to be a fluke. Probably a random ad everyone sees. She shook her head. *You're imagining things. A cell phone can't possibly read a person's mind.* Determining that it was a weird coincidence, the imaginings of her recently sleepy mind, she began to play the new cards dealt in front of her.

Still, Maya found herself deliberately thinking about buying a shovel, or maybe a few other new garden tools, as a sort of test. Gardening was a completely different topic from her throbbing knee, but she expected nothing... hoped for nothing. Mind reading technology wasn't available, she admonished herself.

She continued playing solitaire, drowsing again, then startling when a new ad popped up. It was for a big box store's gardening equipment!

Discomforted, she started climbing out of bed, thinking that she would boot up her computer and research advertising technologies and mind reading. She stopped herself with one leg dangling over the bedside. *No, it's late and that's ridiculous. Mind reading isn't something technology could do. If such a thing was possible, there would be public technology being sold to read minds, like machines for police interrogation, or somebody would be selling a game app called Mind Reading with Friends.*

She snuggled back under the covers, her nerves calming. Not wanting to believe what she'd seen, wanting badly for it to be coincidence, Maya tested the game again. This time, she focused on something she *never* thought about: buying a new car. She loved her old Honda, and she'd never done any searches about replacing it. She pictured the beloved vehicle's dents and dings, waiting to see if a related ad would pop up.

No ads appeared referencing cars, nor vehicles of any type. The game displayed one cat food ad after another, with litter and cat toy ads interspersed. That made sense, at least, and she relaxed, banishing all thoughts of mind-reading cell phones. *I'm just tired. Certainly, this thing can't read my mind!* She harrumphed at her attempts to summon car ads... conveniently forgetting about the joint medicine and gardening tools

advertisements. Her mind settled as she continued playing the game, and Maya drifted off to sleep.
***

Several evenings later, tucked up in bed with the heavy comforter encasing her, Maya played solitaire and hoped to soon doze. Her mind relaxed, eyelids drooping, and her fingers slowed, often missing cards, as sleep approached.

Somewhere in the back of her mind, a thought drifted forward. She remembered the joint pain ad and realized that she hadn't seen it since. She'd forgotten the name of the medicine; her knee was better, anyway. What she *was* seeing on the screen was an advertisement for a local auto painting and body shop, mingled among the cat-related ads. She dismissed the auto shop ad quickly, disturbed by it, and more awake than she'd been a moment before.

She set aside the phone and stared at the bedroom ceiling. Pulling at the comforter, she wrapped it close around her. Maya didn't want to believe that the game on her smart phone, or the phone itself, could determine her thoughts. The latest ad was way too relevant, though. It was not a car sales ad, although that was what she'd been deliberately thinking at the cell phone to "test" it a few days ago; it was a body shop that could knock out the dents and dings she'd inadvertently pictured in her mind during that test.

She scooted sideways under the comforter and reached for her smart phone. Picking it up, she powered the phone down. If she missed a call, then she missed a call. That could be dealt with in the morning. Right now, though, Maya didn't want her cell phone reading her mind.

She didn't want it to know that she had become aware of what it was able to do.

One New Voicemail

Annie stared at her smart phone. After the police had left, after she'd called her brothers and sisters and they'd cried for their mother, she'd seen the voicemail notification. She'd played the voicemail, then played it again. And again.

Annie heard the front door open as the voicemail played a fourth time. She stopped it and walked to the door to greet her arriving siblings.

Their mother died in a car accident that morning. Annie invited them to come by and help her with arrangements, and all of them had come. They stood in the entry way, trading hugs and sobbing.

The youngest, Amelia, held onto Annie like a sloth gripping a branch. "We're orphans now, Annie," she cried.

Annie moved her sister until she was in a side hug and one arm was free. Holding her cell phone aloft, Annie said, "There's something you all need to hear."

The three others followed Annie, Amelia still clinging to her side, into the living room. Helping her young sister to sit, Annie freed herself with help from their brother, Alan, who held Amelia in place and patted her back.

Annie connected her smart phone to a wireless speaker. She cranked the volume high and played the voicemail she'd received from their mother.

They listened, shocked.

"Play it again," her brother Adam said. She did.

They listened again. Annie cocked her head, her ear close to the speaker, asking herself if maybe a bystander got to Mom before the paramedics' loud approach. But, in her heart she knew that wasn't the case.

Adam walked across the room to Annie and held his hand out for her phone. She placed it in his palm, then squeezed his arm before he stepped away.

He started the recording at the halfway point, after the good-bye message from their mother, to where Mom's dying breath ended and was followed by a brief silence.

Then, that distinctive voice came through the speakers again. Adam backed up the voicemail and hit Play. Listening, Annie recognized their father's voice clearly. Adam sat on the couch opposite Annie, backed up to the beginning again and leaned over the speaker, listening intently.

Annie examined each face around the room. She knew that they all recognized Dad's voice too.

This time, Adam let the voicemail run through to the end. Their father's voice was followed by minutes of silence before the sounds of the paramedics arriving blasted through the speaker.

"You hear Dad, right?" asked Alice, the middle sister.

Annie, Adam, Amelia, and Alan nodded in unison.

Adam played the recording several more times, as they wept and took turns patting Amelia on the back.

"So, Mom's with Dad now," Amelia said with finality. "That makes me feel better."

Annie wiped her eyes and smiled. What a cleansing thought that was. She didn't feel like crying anymore, and a laugh escaped her.

***

The day of their mother's funeral, the siblings gathered again with a wide swath of family and friends joining them. The church pews were packed. The pastor spoke. Everyone sang Mom's favorite hymn, *Amazing Grace*. Then the pastor called for family to come up and speak.

Annie and Adam took the stage together. Annie said, "After the car crash, Mom left me a voicemail telling us goodbye and that she loved us. We'd like to share it with you."

She walked over to the church's sound system control board, where her phone was already set up. Adam said a few words asking everyone to brace themselves, as Mom's final breath would be hard for them to hear, but that this voicemail was important for them to share. It was a joyous message, not sad, Annie heard Adam explain.

Annie had the voicemail set to start playing at their mother's first words, and Annie was poised to stop it before the first responders could be heard. She hit Play and her mother's voice resonated from the church speakers.

> *Annie.* (A pant.)
>
> *Annie, honey, I've been in a car accident.* (A pause.)
>
> *Kiddo, I'm hurt. I'm sure I'll see you at the hospital but* — (A groan.)
>
> *But honey, I want to just say I love you. Please tell your sisters and brothers I love them too. I LOVE YOU ALL!* (More panting.)
>
> *I'm hurt but I'm okay* (said in a reassuring voice, and Annie thought she heard a forced smile with these words).

I love you guys. We have a good life, guys. You guys did so well after your Dad died, and I know you'll be okay. (No more reassurances about seeing her at the hospital.)

I'm not in any pain, kiddos. I just want you to know— (Coughing.)

Oh my god. (A pause.)

Oh, sweetheart! (A deep, last breath.)

(A brief silence.)

Then, their Dad's voice came through the speakers, "You're okay, sweetheart. I've got you. Welcome."

Annie stopped the voicemail. She didn't want the congregation to hear the paramedics yelling back and forth, saying, "she's gone," and "man, this car is crushed," nor hearing one of the first responders picking up Mom's phone and saying, "Hello, hello," before ending the call — and the voicemail message.
Unexpectedly, the congregation erupted. The mix of tears and screams surprised Annie. She looked to the pulpit and saw the shock on Adam's face. Neither of them expected this chaos. Nor what came next.
"Lord, take me!" a woman shouted. The pastor ran to her and as he tried to calm her, she shouted it again.

***

Later, as the police left — having responded to the melee inside and outside the church — the siblings stood numbly on the church steps.
"This is about Mom and Dad," Anna said softly. "I don't understand why everyone was screaming."

She and her siblings couldn't foresee that the weeks to come were to bring droves of suicides and congregations drinking poisoned wine together.

Their evidence of the afterlife, which had brought them such solace, sent others running toward it.

Long Shadows

The old man rocked, the chair creaking a rhythmic lullaby to him. He watched, otherwise silent, as the trees' shadows spread across the lawn, silhouette fingers crawling forward as the sun approached the horizon.

Edgar Mills had lived at Long Shadows all his life. He'd grown up in the big house, his father working for the Anderson family. When he'd been old enough, he'd helped his Dad, and that led to his gaining a job assisting the gardener, then to his taking over his father's job upon Dad's retirement.

Now Edgar was retired, a spry 80, and still here. He'd been with the family for so many decades that the owner provided him a small room in which to live out his days; a private, cozy — bordering on claustrophobic — room down the hall from the kitchen and a few steps from the gardens outside.

Here on the screened porch Edgar rocked every evening, always when the shadows began their creeping. Their movements mesmerized him.

No matter how the trees were trimmed, topped, or butchered each fall, their shadows took the form of fingers edging across the lawn. One year when Edgar was middle-aged, the property owner — middle-aged himself at the time — ordered a swath of trees to be removed. Mr. Anderson's bedroom window facing the lawn played a part in the order for clear-cutting; that's what Edgar had thought at the time, and still believed.

Although more than a dozen tall oaks were felled, the fingers continued their spider-like motion across the yard; though, Edgar had noted, the shadow hands seemed more pronounced than they were prior to the cutting. Mr. Anderson then ordered thick, black-out curtains that muddled his well-appointed bedroom suite, but prevented him from seeing outside unless he chose to see. He didn't. According to the cleaning staff, the heavy curtains hadn't been opened since their installation.

As Edgar rocked, the shadows marched forward. Once the sun set, the shadow-hands would melt into the darkness, expanding to envelope the house and grounds. Edgar, along with his chair, would be blotted out, save for the glow emitting from inside where kitchen lights shone brightly. Somewhere in the house, Edgar knew the only other nighttime worker toiled. Marianne, who headed the cleaning staff and had been recently widowed, tended to the family's needs. Her husband had, too, until his death. Now she cared for ailing Mr. Anderson.

Like Edgar, Marianne had been given a little room of her own — it was one of few kindnesses Edgar had seen Long Shadows' owners, the Anderson family, show to their employees.

As old as Edgar, the current Mr. Anderson, Benjamin, was the final member of his family line — and as such was painfully aware of the shadows. The legend, as it were, was that these unique shadows would continue to the end of the last Anderson's life. Still, recently Mr. Anderson had met with the grounds crew and enlisted them in covering the lawn with an orchard full of fruit trees. These, he'd said, would provide shade and pleasant foodstuff for his final years.

Edgar knew the owner of Long Shadows didn't give a fig about figs, or apples, or any of the other fruit trees he'd commissioned. He knew Mr. Anderson's secret goal was to halt the terrifying shadow-fingers that tormented him at each sundown.

The fruit-trees plan was sure to fail, Edgar thought; but if it succeeded, *he* would miss the shadows. They were a part of the place. Long before his birth, and throughout his eighty years of life, the shadows had gripped the property each evening. He'd feared them as a child, until his father explained that only the Andersons need fear them. This had comforted young Edgar and stopped him playing with Benjamin Anderson — who was his same age. In his adult life, Edgar came to understand it to be viewed as a curse upon the family. From what he had seen, it was more karma than curse, and deserved.

When Edgar had grown older, during a bout of illness Mr. Anderson had feverishly confided to Edgar that he feared being taken away by clasped fingers at his end. If the family legend was true, they would come for Mr. Anderson. Edgar believed it was true. Planting fruit trees wouldn't stop that.

Edgar Mills rocked, the chair resuming its song. The wind was beginning to blow, and he heard the grass rustling. Off in the distance, night birds called. He thought he heard an owl hoot, followed by a shrill shriek. *Something has caught its dinner*, he thought.

He watched the shadows seem to pinch at the ground as they stretched over the green lawn. Peering toward the woods in the embers of the day, he made out a set of white wings. The wings disappeared into the darkness under the trees. Soon, everything would be within the shadowy grip.

Lightening flashed unexpectedly. Edgar had been watching the shadows and not noticed the overcast sky. When the lightening flashed again, he saw fast-moving clouds spreading as far as he could see.

Edgar heard footsteps go past the screen door behind him. He turned in his chair; its rhythmic rocking ceased momentarily, and he caught a glimpse of Marianne walking toward the kitchen.

He resumed rocking. Hearing her speaking, he turned around in the rocking chair as far as he could, and in his old voice yelled, "What's that, Miss Marianne?" A moment later, he realized she wasn't speaking to him, but to someone on the phone. Rolling thunder covered her words.

He returned to his rocking. From inside, the house phone returned to its cradle with a thump-ring, and her footsteps grew louder. He looked over his shoulder as Marianne pushed the screen door open and joined him on the porch. As soon as she released the door, she wrung her hands.

"What's wrong, miss?" He thought he knew already.

Wringing her hands hard enough to turn her knuckles white, she said, "Mr. Anderson is still unwell. He tells me he feels fine, but his temperature keeps going up. I just took it, and it's over 104 degrees!"

Edgar rose and patted her back to comfort her. Her long gray hair was pulled tight at the sides, held back by a wide barrette she always wore. Two feet of rippling curls trailed from the back of her head and under his patting hand. He tried to recall when she and her now-dead husband had arrived at Long Shadows. Back then, her hair had been chestnut, her face free of wrinkles. *She can't have been here more than 20 years*, he thought, *but she's aged much more than that during her time here.*

"I've called for an ambulance," she whispered.

He patted softly on her back again, her curls bouncing under his touch, and he withdrew his hand in embarrassment.

She was a taken woman, after all, even if her soulmate wasn't there to remind Edgar.

"Let me get you a nice hot cup of coffee while we wait," Edgar said. Opening the screen door, he gently pushed her inside and followed. The snap of the door into its frame behind them was followed by a thunderclap — close enough that Edgar flinched. Marianne gasped, jumped three inches from the floor and came down flailing, Edgar grabbing at her elbow to keep her on her feet.

"Steady now," he said as she nodded her thanks. He kept hold of her elbow until they reached the kitchen, where he helped her take a seat at the staff table. Marianne's hands resumed their wrestling as he filled two cups with steaming coffee.

As she took the cup from him, her hands finally rested. She didn't drink, instead looking up the stairs toward the second floor, where Mr. Anderson was.

"Has the nurse come by to see him today?"

Marianne shook her head, her eyebrows drawing together over her scowling face. "No," she spat. "She hasn't been here for a week. It's shameful."

"The nurse should have come. I understand your being upset. Likely, miss, there was nothing they could have done for him that you haven't done. It's his time, I believe, and it's good you've cared for him as you have."

"Thank you for saying that," she whispered. Her taut face relaxed, her eyebrows returning to worry-position as she let her anger go.

Edgar glanced out the window. The porch was all but obliterated by the evening shadows. "Finish your coffee, and I'll go up with you to see him."

***

As they walked into Mr. Anderson's expansive bedroom, the heavy curtains, rod and all, fell to the floor with a clatter. He clutched at her arm reflexively. Thick shadows pressed through the windows and across the ceiling until they hovered over Mr. Anderson's bed. The supine man cried out.

"It's all right, sir," Edgar said, walking quickly toward the bed. Marianne beat him there.

Outside, the ambulance's siren blared. Marianne turned as if to go downstairs to let them in, and Edgar grasped her hand. He shook his head at her. "They can wait a moment. Let's stay with Mr. Anderson. You can open the door for them soon."

Edgar let go of her hand and Marianne stepped closer to the bed. She gently wrapped both her hands around Mr. Anderson's hand. Edgar moved to the other side of the bed and placed his hand on the dying man's shoulder. They stood silently; the sound of his last few breaths filling the room as the bedroom darkened.

A moment later, the room brightened as normal. No shadows remained across the ceiling. Edgar checked for a pulse but knew the owner of Long Shadows was dead.

"You can let them in now, miss. He's gone, but they'll have to see him."

***

The ambulance drove away empty, leaving the departed Mr. Anderson to the mortician, and the hearse parked at the bottom of the house's long stone staircase. Any moment now, Edgar knew the mortician and his assistants would come out with Mr. Anderson's body, and take him away from Long Shadows for good. Not even his ashes would return.

Another car rolled up the long drive. Edgar recognized it; the family trustee coming to oversee removal of the last Anderson family member.

Marianne wiped her nose, sniffed, and gave Edgar a forlorn look. "The shadows... does that mean he... he's not gone to heaven, has he?"

Edgar looked down for a moment, then sighed. "I don't know for certain, miss. We can't know for certain. You know I grew up with him here. I know who he was, the things he'd done. You know some too, I expect, as you've been here for some years." The old man pinched his nose, surprised to find tears on his fingertips. "Whatever he'd done, you and I did the only thing that we could, which was comfort him. We showed him kindness at the end, and you should be content in that, miss. What happens to him now, wherever he is, well, he's earned it, hasn't he?"

They stood in silence, the moon bright overhead, as an owl called from the yard. Far into the woods, a tree fell, followed by another, then another. Edgar knew that the fingerlike shadows would never cross the property again.

Miss You

The woman slowly lowered her legs off the bed and sat upright. She didn't feel ready to face the day. The past weeks of coughing, chills, and sweating had worn her down. Plus, today was an unwanted anniversary. Her husband had passed away a year ago today, and her heart ached extra for it. His name was Lee. Her name was Leigh Ann.

Shuffling into the kitchen, Leigh Ann stood looking at the coffee pot and thinking of the mornings the two of them had shared over coffee. After a moment, she gripped the pot and moved it to the sink, then watched it slowly fill with water. She felt clear-headed as she went through the steps — pour water into the coffee maker reservoir, add filter and coffee grounds, hit the brew button — that she hadn't been able to think through until today. She'd been muddled since the infection had knocked her down and no tasks had been easy.

Hazy moments drifted across her mind, sunlit and nighttime moments blended, lost in fever. Throughout it all, his ghost had been with her. She felt sadness at knowing that with recovery she could no longer see across the veil.

Shuffling into the living room, Leigh Ann sat on the empty couch, the only sound the coffee maker gurgling. She drew her computer toward her, brushing dust off the keyboard absentmindedly. She perused the usual word-war on Twitter and memes on Facebook, then went to her own Facebook timeline and posted: *A year today. Miss you, sweetheart.*

A few minutes later as she was pouring coffee into her mug, the phone rang. She returned the pot to the coffee maker and lifted the cell phone from the counter. The display showed it was her mother calling. Not quite feeling ready to talk, she answered anyway. "Hi, Mom."

"Oh, it's so good to hear your voice! You must be feeling better. It's been days since you've been on Facebook. How are you feeling? Are you still running a fever? Are you sure you're feeling well enough to be up?" Her mother never stopped long enough for her to answer any question. Then her mom asked, "I saw your post. What was a year ago? Who are you missing?"

She was about to respond — angry at her mother's forgetfulness of the date's importance — when she heard the front door unlock. It swung open and she watched, agape, as Lee walked in carrying a shopping bag.

"Good morning," he said sweetly, "I went to get that flavored creamer you like. I figured if you had your appetite back, you might want something special." He dropped the bag on the kitchen counter, adding, "Sorry I didn't leave a note. I thought I'd be back before you woke up."

She dropped the cell phone. It clattered onto the counter as she realized her grief had been a fevered nightmare. She hugged him hard as her mother's voice shouted more questions from the still-connected phone.

Freya's Friend

"Please, Mommy, I want to sleep over here with my friend." Freya begged, her eyes pleading with puppy-level effectiveness.

Freya's mother, however, didn't fold. She stared at the four-year-old with more confusion than surrender. "What friend, sweetheart?"

Freya patted the wall against which she was leaning. Her lower body wrapped in her sleeping bag, a pillow beside her, she held her arm against the wall with her right hand flat. Brown eyes still anchored to her mother's eyes, her curly chestnut hair cascaded down the wall. "My friend here," she said.

As the tall woman took a step backward, Freya asked, "Where are you going, Mommy?"

"Nowhere," Mommy said, barely a whisper. She cleared her throat. "Your friend *where*?"

"Here," Freya said more emphatically, patting her palm against the wall several times. "You know my friend, don't you? He's lived here all my life. You have to."

Mommy shook her head. "I don't... understand," she responded, haltingly.

Freya huffed. "This is why I liked my bed here, Mommy. I didn't want you to move it over there." Freya removed her arm from the wall and pointed across her bedroom, shaking her head so hard that her dark curls danced. They cast a shadow on the wall that raised goosebumps on her mother's arms.

Stepping forward, her mother knelt beside the girl's sleeping bag. "Do you mean you have an invisible friend? You need to go sleep in your bed. You'll be more comfortable, and your friend can join you."

Mommy shivered as Freya shook her head obstinately, and said, "He's not invisible, and he can't go that far." The four-year-old hugged herself with both arms, defiance flashing in her eyes. "I always sleep by my friend."

Gulping back her misgivings, she asked her daughter, "Can you tell me about your friend, Freya?" She stroked her daughter's hair and the girl ducked away, bonking her head softly against her hair shadow on the wall.

Freya relaxed. "Sure. His name is Brian, and he's my friend. I thought he was my brother, like Freddie is, but he isn't. He lived here when we moved here, but I was too little then, so he told me about it. He is five years old, and he doesn't get older like I do on my birthdays. Next year I'm gonna be five like him." The girl paused as her mother's hand hovered above her hair again. Freya cocked her head, moving out of range of the offending hair stroker, and looked quizzically at her mother.

Mommy smiled, at least with her mouth. Freya thought her eyes looked funny, but continued brightly, "He can't leave the wall, so I keep him company." She nodded her head once, punctuating what she thought was a complete explanation.

After a long silence, Freya's mother patted her head again, then leaned in and kissed her forehead. "You sleep here for tonight, and we'll talk about this more tomorrow." She kissed her daughter's cheek, fluffed the sleeping bag around Freya as she scooted prone onto the floor. With a final pat on

Freya's head as she nestled onto the pillow, her mother dashed from the room.
***

The following Saturday, Freya's mother — in actuality, Mariah Forrester — waved good-bye to her daughter and son from the front door. Her husband Sam's parents were taking the children for the day, and for a night — although the children didn't yet know that.

"Ready?" Mariah jumped as Sam spoke from behind her.

"Ready," she confirmed.

The two marched into Freya's bedroom. "Are you sure about this?" Sam asked, staring at the wall.

"No, but she is so sure this little boy is there, and never anywhere else."

"You're sure this is the spot where her friend is?" Sam asked, touching the wall, then quickly withdrawing his hand, and shaking it, Mariah noticed.

"I'm sure. Believe me, I listened to her carefully and she said the same thing every time. Last night, she asked me to put my hand on the wall and it felt... cold." She pointed at the wall, shuddering. "She's been in that sleeping bag on the floor for the last five nights."

"It's really cold. This is so weird," Sam said.

"I know."

Sam left the room and returned with a toolbox and level. Mariah began marking cut lines on the drywall, as Sam plugged in the power saw. Soon they would see first-hand Freya's "friend" who lived inside the wall.
***

Sam ended the phone call. "My parents understand. I gave them our hotel name, and they'll keep the kids at their house until Monday. My mom's a little freaked out, but they won't tell Freddie and Freya anything."

"Good." Mariah slung her backpack onto her shoulders. "I'm all set. Let's go before they pull that poor little boy's body out of the wall."

Didn't have to tell Sam twice. He grabbed his bag and followed his wife to the car, nodding to the police officer by the door.

Driving to the hotel, Mariah asked, not for the first time, "Are you sure they'll lock up when they leave?"

Sam sighed, but smiled. "Yes. They promised they'll lock up, and chances are they'll be in our house for a while tonight, then back tomorrow. I told that guy in charge, Detective what's-his name--"

"Arthur," she interjected.

"Yeah, Detective Arthur. He knows where we're staying, and he said they'll be done by tomorrow at the latest. We can put the wall back tomorrow night, Detective Arthur promised."

"Good."

Sam pulled into a parking spot at the Moonlight Hotel — a throwback at which under other circumstances they would not have stayed — and Mariah gasped. She looked at Sam, wide-eyed. "What are we gonna tell Freya when she finds out her friend is gone?"

Taking Notes

Madilyn had written enough mystery stories that, while listening to Lisa tell her tale of innocence to the detective, she recognized the lie.

An unmarked police car had appeared just as the writers' club's monthly luncheon was starting; Lisa was hosting at her home this week. Detective Reynolds showed his badge at the door and explained solemnly that Lisa's estranged husband had been found, presumably murdered, in his west-coast home. The detective questioned each club member, ending with Lisa.

Lisa had told the detective that she had gone to the store that morning. But Madilyn had seen her arrive and let them all inside. Lisa hadn't been carrying anything. Madilyn noted the discrepancy to an imaginary notebook inside her head.

The club members were given permission to leave soon after, the detective and his partner remaining inside with Lisa. The group filed out and went to their cars, for once, wordlessly.

Madilyn was about to start her car when a glimmer of color caught her eye. She glanced toward the house to make sure no one was watching, then stepped out of the car and lit a cigarette to give the impression she was hanging around only to smoke.

She cautiously approached Lisa's car where a bright orange bit of something was stuck to the fender. She didn't touch it; instead, she returned to her car and stood puffing slowly, hoping the detective would come out soon.

Detective Reynolds appeared as Madilyn snubbed out the cigarette. She nodded as he approached. He cocked his head sideways, then walked to where Madilyn stood.

"Was there something you wanted to add?" he asked.

"No, just having a smoke before I start driving. Safety first!" Madilyn said far too loudly. The detective gave her a strange look as Madilyn waved to Lisa standing inside the screen door. Lisa slammed her front door without returning the wave.

In a low voice, Madilyn told the detective that she had seen something and pointed to Lisa's car. She then climbed into her car and drove away.

In her rear-view mirror, Madilyn saw the detective circling the car. He pulled the orange thing from the fender and dropped it into a bag. Madilyn made her turn onto the road and headed home.

***

At the next month's writers' club luncheon — it was Madilyn's turn to host — no one spoke of the police investigation. Instead, they vigorously discussed their latest projects.

Lisa had elected to read a poem that she said was being published in an upcoming children's book. Each of the club members congratulated her. After she'd read it aloud, they gave Lisa suggestions, which to Madilyn meant that each had found fault with her poem. *And no wonder*, Madilyn thought. She found the poem ghastly. In it, a living pumpkin had its innards eaten by a dog as a black cat laughed. Madilyn shuddered at the horror. It wasn't a poem Madilyn would read to *her* grandchildren! She had kept her opinion to herself but wondered at the poem's violent imagery. She jotted another note in her imaginary notebook.

***

A week passed. The evening before the next writers gathering — assuming they'd still meet — Madilyn sat down to edit her latest chapter so that she might have a suitable excerpt to read to the group. It was a mystery novel, and in it she planned to have the murderer exposed by an observant flower shop operator who happened to be engaged to a detective. She'd described the shopkeeper as *Sherlock-esque*, with her detective fiancé contributing as a kind of Watson — but one who took all the credit when the shopkeeper wasn't within earshot.

Her mind wandered from her fiction, though, and she stared out the window at the night beyond. Madilyn wondered if, as Lisa appeared to be a clumsy murderer, then perhaps her murderer in the novel was too clever.

Clumsy or not, she mused, Lisa was still free. By this time Madilyn's imaginary notebook page was full of clues she'd logged by reviewing her previous interactions with Lisa. The police would have more, she hoped. If not... well, maybe Madilyn could talk with the detective who had questioned them on the day Lisa's soon-to-be-ex-husband was murdered. *Found murdered*, Madilyn corrected herself. She didn't remember Detective Reynolds saying how long he had been dead.

But how did she do it? Madilyn mused. She tried to imagine the sequence of events. Lisa would have had to travel thousands of miles to the wilds of Washington state. She'd had to have killed her estranged husband, and then driven all the way back. Something must have gone a bit wrong for Lisa to have arrived home late for the writers' club gathering. Madilyn and two others had already arrived when Lisa came down the driveway. With no bags from the store, she recalled, confirming that fact was on her mental list.

Madilyn decided that she would go and see the detective. That was the appropriate thing to do, she assumed, when one has information the police might not have. She smiled as she envisioned herself as a writer detective, like the heroine of her favorite TV show.

***

The next morning when she stepped through the police station door, however, she immediately felt embarrassed. *They're the experts*, she thought. *Maybe I shouldn't suppose that my observations will be helpful.*

"Yes, what do you need?" asked a uniformed officer standing behind a counter with a clear plastic barrier. Madilyn's face flushed. She shyly approached and asked to speak to Detective Reynolds. "He's on his way in now. Take a seat," the officer said sternly. Madilyn did as she was told, her embarrassment being joined by an irrational fear that she was in trouble.

While she waited, Madilyn examined the feeling and the emotions she felt, thinking that she might use them for a character in her mystery novel. Shame reared its ugly head as she thought how this experience with Lisa's murdering might improve the quality of her writing. She flushed visibly, and covered her face, lest she get in more imaginary trouble with the police.

She heard the police station door open and looked up. Detective Reynolds walked purposefully past the counter and toward the stairs. Madilyn stood, calling his name.

He turned, saw Madilyn, and stopped in his tracks. He stood waiting for her to come to him. "Hello, sir," Madilyn said. "I wanted to tell you something."

He sighed audibly. "I remember you. Do you know something about Lisa Hardy and her husband?"

"Well, no," Madilyn said haltingly. "I've noticed a few things and, well, I feel it's my duty to share them--"

"God save me from amateur detectives," he said, not under his breath; it echoed and heads turned across the room.

Madilyn flushed, muttered an apology, and turned to leave.

"Wait," Detective Reynolds said. She stopped, her face red with embarrassment and humiliation. "Come and tell me. I have the time anyway." Another sigh.

She followed him upstairs where he directed her toward a scruffy chair next to his desk. He sat and reached into a pile of papers covering the majority of the desktop. He withdrew a file folder. Balancing it on top of the mess, he flipped it open, and lifted a piece of paper. "This is a report I received yesterday. That orange thing on Mrs. Hardy's car was bark from a tree that we don't have here. It grows in the northwestern US, where Mrs. Hardy's husband was living. Where he was killed. It will be hard for her to explain how it got stuck in her fender from hundreds of miles away."

Madilyn took the report from him, nodded her thanks, and sat down in the well-used plastic chair provided. She pulled her cell phone from her pocket and searched for the tree listed in the report: Pacific Madrone. Instantly, photos and links appeared showing trees with bright orange, peeling bark.

"That bark is distinctive," the detective said. "I'm waiting for a DNA check on a tree the detectives out there discovered by Mr. Hardy's driveway. Thank you for pointing it out to me." This last, he murmured.

Madilyn's embarrassment faded away. "You're welcome," she said loudly, feeling vindicated.

Rolling his eyes, he asked Madilyn, "So what did you come here to tell me?"

Madilyn flipped open the imaginary notebook in her head. She rattled off the list of clue-like information she'd gathered. When she finished, she stared at him.

He was staring back, his eyes saucers. Finally, he said, "Okay. Thank you for coming in." He rose and motioned her away.

Madilyn left. *Jerk*, she thought, followed by harsher words.

***

That evening Madilyn saw a headline on a local news site indicating that "Local Author Lisa Hardy" had been arrested and was suspected in the murder of her estranged husband. Madilyn gasped, then giggled delightedly — to her own horror.

She read the article twice. It contained details of the crime and the names of the Washington state detectives. It said nothing about evidence, to which she pouted. It didn't name Detective Reynolds either. Madilyn took satisfaction in that. *No fame for surly Detective Reynolds,* she thought, recognizing that she was being petty. She noted that in her upcoming mystery novel, she should avoid transferring such a pettiness to her beloved mystery-solving character.

Suddenly, realization hit her that her writer-friend Lisa was in jail. She felt a range of emotions and examined them, taking physical notes with a nearby pencil and notebook. Then thoughts of her friend's dire situation passed, and she began selfishly wondering if she could question Lisa on how she felt about being arrested, or even how she felt while committing the murder.

Then, it struck her that she had found a key piece of evidence —the incriminating orange bark — and Madilyn squealed with delight at the thought that she might be called as a witness in Lisa's trial. Certainly, Lisa would never speak to her again, so questioning her was off the table; but the thought that she might experience court from the witness box offered quite a wonderful opportunity to gain court experience. Perhaps she'd learn something that might be used to perk up a character or two in her novel.

***

Many months later, her testimony and all the "bad business" behind her, Madilyn was running late for the club luncheon. She pulled into a parking space and jumped out. The writers' club had begun meeting in public places. *Not wanting to take a chance another murderer was among them,* Madilyn mused. She walked into the pizza joint and waved at the group seated around a large table, then joined them.

The writers ate silently; personal chit-chat had ended with Lisa's conviction. When they'd finished eating, they shared and discussed their latest writing projects, before rushing off to their vehicles.

To home and safety, Madilyn thought as she watched each member drive off.

Sitting at her computer later that afternoon, Madilyn worked on her new novel. This was not a murder mystery; she'd decided to leave that genre behind. Her brief encounter with murder and mayhem, and watching her friend be convicted, had left a bitter taste in her mouth. Yes, her experience on the witness stand had been educational, and maybe one day she'd get over it enough to write it down. It had surprised her, in many deeply examined ways, how she'd disliked her mystery after Lisa was sentenced to death.

Madilyn typed away on her new work, a light-hearted story of a group of wood sprites living in a rainbow-flanked forest far away. This story would be cheery, and she poured into it all of the cheeriness she could muster.

Maybe the trees will have orange bark, she thought, her face greening at the thought.

Beyond the Werewolf

Vic Moriani surveyed the man in the wing-back chair beside him. Murmuring voices surrounded them, the party in full swing. He leaned toward William Bellamy, the leather couch emitting a squeak as he moved to its edge. He said in a voice that would carry, "If what you say is true, that werewolves are real, Bellamy, then why are there no were-dogs? Or were-cats, for that matter? Or, what about were-raccoons? Why doesn't *any* animal bite transform a human into a hybrid of *that* animal?"

William Bellamy sighed exasperatedly. "Because not all animals carry a transforming disease! I said I had heard the local lore about werewolves, and that from the evidence I believe in these wicked beings. That's a far cry from what you're suggesting. No one would put stock in your silly musing."

"What about were-badgers?" Moriani enjoyed taunting the pompous man sitting opposite him. No matter the topic, Bellamy had set beliefs about the world, and nothing and no one could change them. It was Moriani's pleasure to goad him. Certainly, it livened up the otherwise dull party.

Another deep sigh from tuxedo-adorned Bellamy, who sipped from the scotch glass in his hand, then smacked his lips. "As I have explained, only an animal carrying — and transmitting in its bite — a transformative germ can affect humans. Only wolves are known to have such a germ. That is why only werewolves exist, not other were-creatures! Your ramblings are preposterous."

Mischief twinkling in his green eyes, Moriani teased, "Well, by your argument dismissing all other types of animals, what about those in the *canine* family? Why would you believe that wolves are able to spread such a malady, but foxes unable to make were-foxes? If such a disease can exist in one canine--"

"Stop!" Rubbing his eyes and the bridge of his nose, Bellamy bellowed, "Your small talk is ruining what *had* been a delightful party. I've made my beliefs clear, and you're just dragging this on." He sighed, swilling back the last of the scotch and grimacing. "As I've explained, it is because there are no such diseases! Only a werewolf affliction exists, as is plain from local stories going back to our beginnings and is plain from the evidence compiled over centuries. No other animals are known to carry a disease that transforms humans into man-animal hybrids!"

"Are known..." Moriani stressed, tossing Bellamy's words back at him and drawing another sigh from the self-important man. Moriani suppressed a grin with some difficulty as he watched Bellamy's face grow redder.

Moriani placed a look of puzzlement on his own face, then to the further ire of his companion, he mused, "Maybe other animals are sneakier, and thus their human-hybrid transforms are sneakier. Cats can be stealthy, and weasels, or perhaps badgers. What if victims of their bites are likewise transform, but aren't as bumbling as werewolves? Not that wolves are bumblers, mind you, but they are rare enough hereabouts that wolf bites are recognized by their uniqueness. Or perhaps there is evidence only for werewolves because they are big enough to attack large game — giving the afflicted human-wolf transforms large bites. It would be hard for such teeth marks to go unnoticed. But, for all we know, were-cats are attacking smaller prey, and their rampages go unnoticed due to the smaller bites. Don't you agree that this could be the case?"

Bellamy could bear the conversation no more. He stood. "I'm leaving. You and your obsession with animal oddities can blather on as long as you like. There are fools gathered here who may listen, but I am done listening!" He exited the room as he barked the last bit, causing the turn of many elegant heads.

Moriani watched the man go, then felt the cold breeze as the front doors opened, then closed. He nodded politely at the heads still turned toward him.

Moriani set down his drink and shot a sly glance to his partner across the room. Emma Packer shot back a smile — more a Cheshire grin — and nodded. Even across the distance, he could see her long eyelashes batting.

Waiting until he felt certain that Bellamy had driven away, Moriani rose. Straightening his jacket and brushing at his pants — briefly wiping the shiny top of his shoe against a perfectly-creased pant leg, he headed toward the room's broad doorway. He stopped to thank the hosts of the party for "a lovely evening," and continued into the hall.

As he strode across the ornate marble floor, Miss Packer — also formally dressed for the party in a sparkling green floor-length gown to accent the red in her hair — matched his stride and exited beside him. He pulled the door closed behind them and she chuckled. "Oh, Vic. The more you push humans, the more they'll deny."

"Yes, I know, Emma," he replied. "but I enjoy how Bellamy digs in his heels. Shall we dine at his estate again tonight? I'm in the mood for more of his chickens."

"Sounds perfect," she said, a purr in her voice stretching the word.

Moriani grinned and gazed up at the night sky. "The clouds will soon clear if the breeze is any indication. There should be a pretty moon tonight." A light glinted in his eyes, flashing greener than humanly possible.

Stepping into their separate cars, Emma followed Vic as he raced from the parking lot and turned onto the main road. After a mile or so of annoyance at his slow vehicle speed, she zipped past his in her neat convertible. Vic followed, no interest in retaking the lead. He knew where they were going and did not worry when he lost sight of her taillights.

Before long he was parking behind the convertible on the side of a tree-lined road; a shiny white fence on their right backed onto Bellamy's land. Along the road, tree shadows began to show as the moon wrested free of clouds.

He bowed with a flourish as Emma approached him. "I'll follow you to where our dinner awaits."

Emma tucked a small white handkerchief into her driver's side window, hopefully expelling any interest in the two vehicles parked on the side of the road. It would appear to anyone, most of all to those who hated helping others, that she had set up the white flag as a call for assistance, and the car parked behind had already stopped to help her. Everyone would continue driving on. There were too few do-gooders for them to fear anyone *helpful* might chance across their cars, especially at what was now one in the morning.

Moriani's stomach growled. "Who'd have guessed a were-fox like me and a were-badger like you could be such wonderful partners? You make hunting so much easier, my dear."

She purred contentedly, batting her eyes at him in the moonlight. "Not that we exist, mind you."

At that, he laughed boisterously. She shushed him firmly and moved toward the fence.

Side-by-side, and definitely *not* hand-in-hand, the two walked into the trees, over the fence, and onto Bellamy's darkness-soaked estate. Quietly they covered the quarter-mile to where they knew his flocks roamed freely.

To the East, at their backs, lie Bellamy's stables. There, the horses had begun to whinny and stamp in the distance.

As they stepped from under the trees into a clear field, the wind blew back Emma's fiery hair. "The wind is blowing towards us, Vic. The chickens will never know we're coming. Are you ready?"

He nodded and the two partners stood with their faces lifted to the full moon, now hanging in a cloudless sky. Their features began to change. Fur sprouted, blowing back against Emma's loosening dress, and Vic's tuxedo.

Vic could never bear to watch Emma change. She transformed into a were-badger with gangly teeth and black eyes, her head appearing far too small for her body, and he dared not look directly at her, lest he laugh.

For her part, Emma hadn't told him that she found his transformation into a were-fox laughable. As a fox, he had the most jagged teeth she had ever seen. The fur wrapping around his eyes made him look as if he had mere slits.

A few minutes later, they started West across the field; loping across the grass. Soon the two were winding stealthily beneath the trees, moving toward the unaware flock of chickens. At the East side of the field behind them, the horses whinnied crazily, frightened by the scents upon the breeze.

Chickens began to rouse and bock, as two of their number were whisked from their roosts and trundled off into the darkness. No lights turned on in the big house beyond the stables. Vic's face twisted in a foxy smirk, as he thought of the many times Bellamy had re-filled his glass with scotch.

In the morning, Bellamy would discover two of his chickens missing, with no evidence from which to deduce what had carried the hens away.

New in Town

The stranger walked into town mid-morning. The Watchers saw him coming and greeted him as he reached the end of the first block.

"Welcome, young man," said Granger. He was the oldest of the group on-watch, the ones who kept an eye out for newcomers, oversaw town business, and otherwise minimized trouble.

A dozen townspeople joined the Watchers, curious to see the stranger. A new arrival was always a draw.

Lily Watt joined the group. She lived outside of town and was there to drop tomatoes off at the community's provisions shop. The gardens were good this year, and the rural folks shared with town when they could. Allison, the shopkeeper, had been delighted to receive the tomatoes and gave Lily a *Thank You* hug.

The stranger raised his hand in a wave and smiled. "Hello," he responded.

Granger extended his hand, introducing himself. The stranger gripped Granger's hand and shook it, "I'm Billy. Good to meet you, Granger," he said, smiling.

Lily took a step back. She thought that Billy's smile was mismatched to the look in his eyes. As Granger introduced the others, she saw the stranger's eyes darting to each person, then back to Granger. Billy continued smiling as he told them of his long travels and desire for a safe place to sleep.

He's cunning, Lily thought. She looked him over, from his dusty hat down his too-nice-for-the-road clothes, backpack, and hunting boots. Under the dust, his belongings appeared expensive and new, belying his pretense of extensive wandering. *If he's a wanderer*, she thought, *he's sure been finding nice things for himself along the way.* She tried to tell herself that he was probably just good at scavenging, but she knew what she'd seen in his eyes — and that the man had likely acquired his nice things less benignly.

She stepped backward to avoid introduction, then turned and walked away. She thought that the town's Watchers — those on duty and those who'd come on later — might have their hands full with this Billy.

Lily stopped by the honorary Sheriff's office on the way out of town — *honorary* because the Watchers made the decisions. One of their early decisions had been to stop enforcing most laws and just keep the peace, and the Sheriff and his remaining deputies did that. After bringing the Sheriff up-to-speed on the new arrival, with her cautionary assessment shared for good measure, Lily walked him to his car.

She waved as the Sheriff drove off to meet the stranger, riding in one of the few vehicles still in use. She watched as the car glided along the near-empty streets. Other than the group she'd seen meeting the stranger, and the few she knew were in the shop sorting provisions, no human nor animal stirred.

***

Late that afternoon, Lily heard a knock on her front door. She opened it to find one of the Sheriff's messengers. The teen tipped his hat and told Lily he had bad news. She could see his distress. He haltingly explained that a townswoman had been brutalized.

Lily's heart sunk. Her stomach, full of just-eaten tomatoes and bread, gurgled. "Does the Sheriff want me to come?" Lily asked, and the messenger nodded.

Lily thanked the young man and watched as he mounted his horse and jogged off down an adjacent street, off to deliver the Sheriff's message to others.

Lily quickly gathered a few things, readied her horse, and was climbing into the saddle when two neighbors arrived. Rey and Molly rode up and their horses exchanged hellos while Molly filled Lily in on what had happened. The woman attacked was the shopkeeper, Allison Leeds, to whom Lily had delivered tomatoes. Allison was hurt but talking, and she said it was the stranger. There had been a witness too: Allison's adult son had heard his mother shrieking. He walked in, saw what was happening, and knocked Billy unconscious before Allison could be violated.

"They took the man to the Sheriff's office. We're all to meet at town hall," Molly finished.

Lily sighed, then turned her horse and followed Rey and Molly up the road as the sun set. Lost in thought, she didn't notice its beauty. *As if sustaining life isn't hard enough, now we have this*, Lily thought.

Rey sighed and, as if reading her thoughts, he commented, "I could've gone the rest of my life without dealing with this."

Lily and Molly both sighed.
***

Their piece of the world contained a few hundred people who had banded together after the government vaporized and supply trucks stopped rolling. Lily knew them all, including those who'd straggled into town afterward, each finding their place and pitching in. For the most part, people had what they needed to sustain life.

Their last news of violence had come from one town over, where the survivors had turned on each other and ended up in a shoot-out to rival the OK Corral's, decimating that town. Lily dreaded the thought of violence taking hold in their community.

***

When they arrived at town hall, the Sheriff's car, several bicycles, and two horses were outside the building. As Lily dismounted and dropped her reins loosely over a bicycle rack, she felt tears falling. Wiping them away, she straightened, patted her horse, and walked inside with the others.

No one was in the Sheriff's office. They followed candle-flickering down a hallway and into what had been the town hall's council room. There they found the Sheriff, his deputies, and several Watchers, sitting behind the semi-circular council table. Billy was in a chair facing them, flanked by two deputies.

Rey and Molly took seats at the table and Lily leaned against the wall. Lily wasn't officially on-watch this season. She had too many gardens to oversee. Still, the Sheriff had sent the messenger for her. She knew that he valued her advice, and under the circumstances she wanted to have a say. Allison was a friend.

"Okay," the Sheriff stood and began, "This is enough of us. Let's get this going." He cleared his throat and continued, "This man, Billy, arrived in town today and was met by Watchers. They spoke with him, he presented himself as a wanderer. Billy asked Granger for a place to sleep and he was given one. He was fed," the Sheriff motioned toward two

Watchers, a middle-aged couple, indicating that they had provided the meal, "and despite the kindness shown him, he attacked our neighbor, Allison."

The Sheriff sat, and Granger spoke, "You have this opportunity to talk, young man. Having witnesses to your violence, though, I can tell you that you will not be welcome to stay."

After a pause, Billy began speaking, crying crocodile tears, Lily thought, as he blamed Allison. He said that she was flirting, that he hadn't seen a woman in a while, and he was just young. Excuses flowed from his lips like a river.

Lily watched his eyes as he spoke. When Billy's response wound down to blubbering and noisy sobs, she stepped forward and whispered in the Sheriff's ear and he nodded. As Lily stepped back against the wall, the Sheriff said, "Word from the next town over is you hurt someone there too." It was a lie at Lily's suggestion. The Watchers only communicated with other towns once a year. They opened their arms for strangers, but closed their neighborhood off from other burgeoning governments. The community as a whole had decided early-on that they would govern in a new way, discarding the old that had failed so completely.

Billy stiffened, seeming to believe the lie. He said nothing, only bit at his lip. That confirmed to Lily, and those at the council table, that he must have attacked someone else out there beyond their boundary. Otherwise, he would have protested.

Lily took advantage of the quiet moment and asked, "Didn't your parents teach you better?" As Lily spoke, she saw Billy bristle at her mention of 'parents' and she knew his anger was growing. She saw daggers shooting from his eyes.

The air in the room hung heavy with the smell of smoke and candles. Lily heard Billy's quickening breath as he glared at each of them, in turn. Finally, Billy said. "They taught me lots! What's better? Nothings better than anything else, there ain't no right or wrong. You don't know what you're talking about. I'm how the world is," He smiled and his eyes flickered with wickedness.

Lily felt sick in the pit of her stomach. *He's irredeemable*, she thought. She searched inside herself for pity, for empathy for this young man, and found none.

The Sheriff stood, shouting, "All the choices a person can make, and you choose to hurt others?"

"Why not?" Billy said. "The world ended so... *So what* if I do what I want? Everything's free and anybody who doesn't enjoy it is a fool. I bet you're all fools."

Granger cleared his throat and asked softly, "Are you ill or just ignorant, sir?"

"You're ignorant," Billy sneered, looking around the room. "If anybody's sick it's you. I do what I want! Whatever's right for me is right! That's doing the *right* thing. You're dumb *not* to!" He leaned back in his seat, seemingly satisfied by his own words, and clueless to the grim faces around the room.

The Sheriff motioned and Lily saw the deputies beside Billy move closer. *Good instincts*, Lily thought.

Molly spoke up, her voice shaking. "You're being foolish." Her chin jutted up in an unconscious gesture of defiance. Lily saw tears glimmering in Molly's eyes.

"*You're* the fool!" Billy screamed, jumping up from his seat. "And you know what? I'm leaving! I'm moving on. I can go where I want. You yokels got no say over *me*!" He emphasized the word by jabbing his thumb toward his chest.

Billy didn't hear the death knell, but Lily heard its imagined tones and bowed her head.

"Any objections?" Granger asked aloud to the room. Along the council table, Lily heard murmurs of *No* and heard herself saying it.

She raised her head and saw Granger nodding to an older man sitting at the back of the room gripping a small black bag in his hands. The man approached Billy, whom the deputies now held by both arms.

Lily knew, they all knew, what would happen next.

Billy stood, defiantly facing them in his last moment of life.

***

The group walked into the woods together. Each hung their head, but no one cried. The town veterinarian, who had carried out the stranger's death sentence with a syringe, stood back as the Watchers buried Billy's body.

Lily knew that their actions set them as low as the short-sighted stranger. They all knew. They didn't kid themselves. The Watchers' were in place to keep the community as safe as they could, in hope that the next generation might thrive, not just survive. Sometimes it meant doing things they despised.

***

When their task was done, the somber group exited the woods. Lily, walking behind the Sheriff, lifted her head and glanced at a small dogwood tree by the path's end. She knew one of the local deputies was under that tree. He was the first person that the Watchers had "put down." The deputy had been bitter and angry after everything changed. Then, he'd brutally beaten a young man from town — even bragged about it. When this news had reached the recently formed Watchers, they had held a long, soul-chilling meeting. That was the only time the Watchers gave someone a second chance.

A week later, the wayward deputy beat a farmer to death. The Watchers met again. Within hours, the deputy had been dispatched to the dogwood grave.

Lily took a deep breath, then blew it out slowly. She knew they did what they did for the greater good.

She also knew, as she suspected the others all did, that their souls were forfeit.

The Shimmering House

Sophie sat down hard in the reclining chair. Exhaustion flooded through her as she raised her feet, lowered the chair's back, and closed her eyes.

She'd had an early start on the day, with family coming to help her with yard work. She had neglected it since her husband had passed away.

Her nephews installed a locking storm door and four surveillance cameras. Sophie hadn't been sleeping, and her hope was that she might feel safer and be able to rest, rather than jumping at each night noise. Without her husband, she not only felt alone, but unprotected.

Her sister helped her pull weeds and clear the garden. Sophie's youngest daughter visited and planted colorful flowers in the front and back yard flower beds. Together, they'd made the most of the cool spring day. It had been the hardest physical work she'd done in months. It felt good, despite the agony snuggled inside her heart.

Letting out her breath slowly, Sophie sunk into the comfy chair. Swirling her long hair into a loose bun, she tucked the tail through the swirl and pulled it tighten, so it would stay up for a little while without a hair tie. She leaned her head back against the recliner's headrest and peered at the security monitor. Through each camera, she could see flower beds. The rear camera by the new storm door showed flowers in the tidied backyard, and she smiled. She was thankful for the help and prideful of the result. Her husband had always kept the lawn well-groomed, and she thought he'd be happy with how it looked, too.

From her recliner, she watched the security cameras displaying sections of the outdoors on the little monitor. Then, she closed her eyes, sighed, and a wave of relaxation rolled forward and took her. She slept.

***

Sophie awoke to a sound coming from the security monitor. Focusing on its small screen, she saw a rabbit loping through the grass and smiled.

Then, her smile faded. The rabbit was not the only movement. She shook her head and focused on the screen again. Where there should be nothing but newly planted flowers, she saw a shimmering light. For a moment, she feared someone was in her backyard with a flashlight and felt a chill.

The monitor flickered, and when it cleared Sophie saw a small cabin where the light had been. Fully awake now, she moved closer, crouching down with her nose inches from the screen.

The cabin looked old. Its porch was ringed by the flowers planted today and tall roses redder than Sophie had ever seen. She then realized that the roses were growing as she watched.

Leaping up, she ran to the rear window and looked out over the flowers to... nothing. No cabin, no roses. She only saw flowers, grass, and the rabbit.

Running back to the monitor, the cabin glowed. The roses were creeping along the porch and over its roof now. She pushed the record button, but instead of recording, the monitor switched off. She jumped, startled, then pressed the power button and sat on the floor waiting for it to reset.

When the display returned showing all four cameras, Sophie saw only the rabbit, munching on one of her new flowers. While she should have been annoyed, she wasn't. Instead, she felt only relieved that the cabin was not there.

The rest of the evening, Sophie reclined but did not relax. Despite one of her favorite movies showing, she barely watched; her eyes were drawn to the security monitor instead. When the movie ended, Sophie adjusted the camera settings to display only the backyard camera stream, switching off the other three and then setting it to record. She watched it until exhaustion took her, and she again slept.

***

Sun streaming through the blinds awoke Sophie. Achy all over, she crept to the dining room and peered suspiciously out the window. No cabin, just flowers in daylight.

It was just a dream, she told herself.

She didn't make coffee as she normally did. She sat by the window and avoided the living room and monitor. By mid-morning, she had convinced herself that the cabin was all part of a dream.

She steeled herself, walked up to the monitor, and saw only one camera was transmitting, showing the empty backyard. The display was set as she'd "dreamed."

Sophie sat down in the recliner and then, as it had the evening before, the picture shimmered and the brightly lit cabin reappeared. She jumped, lost her balance and slid out of the chair onto the carpet. Crawling on all fours to the rear window, she tentatively looked through the window blinds.

This time, she saw the cabin and the roses clear as day. Their bright petals and dark green leaves glinted in the sunshine. She felt the urge to move closer, to smell the roses.

Sophie found herself in the backyard. She didn't remember unlocking the storm door or walking outside. She hadn't put on shoes and felt soft grass under her feet. Facing the shimmering cabin, she moved close to the porch step, and smelled the scent of the roses. Amazed at their strong perfume, Sophie breathed in deeply, then exhaled.

Without a sound, the cabin door swung open. She knew she should be afraid but wasn't. Through the doorway, she saw someone standing inside. Before the light even hit the figure, she recognized his outline.

She jumped up the step, ran into the cabin, and folded her arms around her husband as the door closed behind them.

***

Sophie's neighbor stood in the doorway, speaking with a police officer. Another officer stood in the living room, looking down at Sophie's body. Sophie lay splayed on the carpet, security monitor clutched in her hand.

"I'd say she's been dead for a day, maybe," the second officer said. "It's a good thing you stopped by, ma'am."

The neighbor hung her head and wept. The first officer put his arm behind her and led her out the front door. "We'll take care of her," he said soothingly. "She's in a better place now."

The Ashes

Maggie finished sweeping the wooden steps and turned to survey the basement. She brushed her wrist across her forehead and it came away wet; she guessed her hair under the head scarf was just as sweaty. *At least I'm almost done*, she thought.

She'd been cleaning since breakfast; the upstairs and ground floor were done. The last bit to tackle was the basement. Technically a basement, it was buried at the front of the house but at ground level with the back yard.

She felt fortunate that, except for the furnace, water heater, and sink, the basement's rooms were empty. In need of a good dusting, yes, but empty. *These three rooms and I'm done.*

The basement didn't have doors, just walls that divided the large area into rooms. One space would become the laundry room — if her brother delivered on his promise to bring her his old washer and dryer. Nicky was one of her *mostly dependable* brothers.

The room along the left side she referred to as the furnace room, and it contained the house's essential equipment, with a funky, too-fancy-for-the-space light fixture above the furnace.

The biggest room, which wrapped around the stairs and along the right wall, she might turn into an art studio... depending on how warm, cold, or humid it was. Maggie had only owned the house for two days, the sale finalized on the first of March, and she had no idea how comfortable any of its parts were going to be. Whatever room she chose to make her art studio would need to be conducive to paint drying and canvas storage. With windows facing into the backyard, she already thought that it felt like an artist's space.

Maggie tugged her mask up from her chin, carefully covering her nose and mouth. Then, she switched from her kitchen broom to a wide push-broom she'd purchased precisely for this job. Maggie brushed down the basement's cinder-block walls, grateful for the mask as the air filled with dust from goodness knows how many decades. She moved slowly, yet the swirling debris never faltered.

When she'd finished the walls, she decided she'd rather vacuum the floor than sweep it. Vacuuming might work better, might not, but her back was twinging and she wanted to avoid stooping with the dustpan.

She hurried up the stairs — the end of the cleaning tunnel visible ahead of her — and dragged the long-necked vacuum to the basement. Her sister Margo had given her the old Oreck ages ago, but after Maggie had cleaned it thoroughly, it had never let her down. Plugging it into a dusty-looking socket, she breathed a sigh of relief when she flipped the on switch and the old appliance started. Quickly she pushed and pulled it across the floor.

It worked better than she'd hoped. When the big room was done, she moved on to the laundry-room-to-be, then carefully dragged the vacuum to the furnace room.

She cringed at discovering a dozen dead bugs jumbled in a corner, aimed the vacuum at them, and watched as bug parts and dust stirred into the air before disappearing into the Oreck.

Despite the ornate overhead light, shadows huddled around the equipment and she moved slowly. *No sense knocking off a hose or otherwise causing myself more work.* Except for the water heater, all the equipment stood several inches from the floor and the vacuum head fit underneath them.

Raising the long neck of the vacuum in the air, she turned to finish the last section. As the vacuum slid behind the water tank, she heard a clink over the Oreck's thrum. She finished the corner with one swipe, then turned off the vacuum, and stooped to see what she'd hit that had made the noise.

Behind the water heater tank she saw a piece of pottery with a smooth top. It was covered in dust, obscuring its color, save for a stripe of blue showing where she'd clinked it. The thought crossed her mind that she was lucky she hadn't broken it. Her cleaning was finished with no broken glass to pick up! "Whew," she said aloud, though the basement managed to muffle it.

Curious, she lifted the blue item and turned it around in her hands. Light dust transferred onto her fingers as she brushed at it, revealing a small metal plate with an inscription: *Alma Tyler (1954-2014)*. She almost dropped it as she realized it was an urn with this person Alma's ashes inside.

She shifted her grip to hold the item firmly in one hand, pressing its top down with her other hand. Then, she retreated from the furnace room and carefully set the urn down on the floor. Making sure it was stable — not wanting to spill ashes, nor make the morally dubious decision to vacuum said spilled ashes — she took a step away. When the vessel didn't tip, she gathered the Oreck and retreated upstairs.

Maggie shoved the vacuum into the deep kitchen pantry, where she knew it couldn't stay long-term, and pushed the door closed to hide the jumble from sight. *All done for today! Time to rest.*

She returned to the basement door, closed it tightly, and turned the key in the lock. Dealing with the urn could wait.

***

Maggie tossed her dusty coverings into a laundry bag and showered, happily releasing her long, chestnut hair from the bonds of the babushka. Not yet thirty years old — although she would be in less than a month — a few gray hairs hid among her dark locks. She didn't mind them; after all, her mother had been completely gray by thirty and Maggie counted herself lucky.

In the shower, she let the hot water wash over her aching muscles. When she finally shut off the water and stepped out, thirty minutes had passed and she noted that the water was still running hot. *The water heater may be ugly, but it does a good job.*

She dressed in her favorite flannel pajamas, grabbed a cheese sandwich from the refrigerator, then relaxed in her upstairs bedroom — as well as she could relax with only an air mattress and laptop computer. The house cleaning was done, the moving van would arrive in the morning, and Maggie kicked back to enjoy the brief lull. A part of her was still in awe of the idea that she owned this house, that 410 Sixth Street, Hope Wells, North Carolina, was all hers.

Knowing the internet wouldn't be connected for several days, she'd brought DVDs along with her change of clothes, chocolate bars, and bags of potato chips. She popped in the first movie and began snacking.

Three movies down, she popped in the fourth, checked the time on her cell phone (3AM), and yawned. Before the new movie's credits rolled, she was asleep.

At 3:30AM Maggie jolted awake. A nightmare of swirling dust continued to play in her mind for a moment as she sat upright on the air mattress. "What the hell was that?"

She struggled to remember the dream. Parts dissipated like smoke as she tried to latch on to them, but some of the dream remained.

It hadn't been dust swirling; it had been ashes. Alma had played a starring role in the bits of the dream Maggie could remember. A faceless silhouette, the old artist had approached Maggie in the dream. Then, Alma's ashes had engulfed Maggie before turning into a hand and squeezing her nose.

"I got your nose!" The old voice had laughed, and the laugh had awoken Maggie.

Wide awake now, she rubbed her nose as if it had been tweaked.

***

Arrival of the moving truck woke Maggie the second time. Her cell phone showed that it was 9AM. She'd slept well after the odd dream, which surprised her. There wasn't time to revisit the images now, though, as she had furniture to move.

She opened the front door as the movers reached it, then blocked it open wide. Scanning the street, her brow furrowed as she saw that none of her siblings had yet arrived. To the "Sure, I'll help," she'd heard from each of them, she had responded with thanks and a start time of 9AM. Knowing them as she did, though, she guessed one or two would arrive within the hour, with the rest trickling in around noon — with hopes that the work was almost done — but Maggie would buy them pizza anyway. As long as she kept *her* word, she was happy. They owned their own shortcomings.

Family. Well, she loved them anyway. Mostly.

Tumultuous hours followed. The movers carried furniture and boxes upstairs without complaint, while Maggie directed placement downstairs. On the ground floor, she stacked boxes in every closet until they overflowed, then piled boxes in corners behind furniture. Each sibling arrived as predicted, with Nicky and Margo being most helpful, while the other three showed up when the truck was nearly empty, and wandered aimlessly carrying small boxes.

Before she knew it, she was waving good-bye to the movers and the house looked better than she'd hoped. The movers had taken care with the furniture; so much so that Maggie had no adjusting to do. The living room was damn near tidy as she and her siblings enjoyed the pizza she'd ordered.

***

When everyone finally left, including Margo who wouldn't stop opening boxes to snoop, Maggie walked around the upstairs. Both the master and the guest rooms had furnishings positioned better than she could have done herself, with dressers and bookshelves in places she wouldn't have even thought to put them. Someone had even deflated the air mattress and it was rolled up in the corner, her laptop carefully placed on top of a dresser nearby. She counted herself lucky and made a mental note to write the moving company a glowing review online… as soon as she got WiFi going.

She remembered that the urn was still in the basement and needed to be dealt with. Jogging down to the first floor, she unlocked the basement door, and descended the stairs. Maggie walked to the urn and bent down to pick it up, then paused without touching it as her dream returned to mind.

What was that crazy dream all about? Sure, an urn with somebody's ashes in it was a weird find, but she had seen urns before. Her dad's ashes had been in an urn on her mom's mantle for the past ten years. What was it about Alma's ashes that had caused her to dream about them?

Who was this Alma? Maggie's internet service would be set up in a day or two. Then, she could search Alma's name, and check out the house's previous owners, to learn more about the abandoned urn and its occupant.

"I think you should just stay here tonight," she said to the urn, then straightened — groaning slightly as her back creaked — and climbed up the stairs.

She locked the basement door and headed into the living room to clean up her house's first mess: pizza plates her siblings apparently couldn't carry to the kitchen trash can.

***

Settling onto her freshly made bed that evening, she opened her email program before remembering that she didn't have internet connected yet. She was about to set her laptop aside when she noticed WiFi networks available. She scanned them, and saw one named, "The Coffee Haus Guest." She'd seen the coffee shop bearing that name, which was just at the end of the block. She clicked to connect, and within seconds was online.

Maggie forgot about wanting to read her email and opened the browser. She first searched for *Alma Tyler, Hope Wells, North Carolina,* on a genealogy site, and was disappointed by the large number of "Tyler" entries.

Browsing to the local newspaper's website, she searched for Alma Tyler, and quickly found an archived obituary: *Alma Robinson Tyler, died peacefully March 20, 2014 at home.* It included a photo of a young Alma and read that she'd been an artist. The obituary listed Alma's address; it was the same as Maggie's new home. *Survived by her nephew, Robert Winstead*, it read.

Mr. Winstead was the man from whom Maggie had purchased the house. *He left his aunt's ashes in the basement,* she thought, disgusted. *Who leaves their aunt's ashes in a basement? Especially when he inherited this house from her!* This was beyond basic jerkiness.

She looked up tax records for her home and found her purchase, a record of transfer to Robert the year Alma died, and Alma's purchase of the home back in 1983 when she was twenty-nine — the same age Maggie was now.

Searching local news again, she found a photograph of a white-haired Alma in front of a mural that the artist had painted in downtown Hope Wells. The mural covered the side of a two-story building and from what Maggie could tell from the part visible in the photograph, the mural depicted a farm field. She wanted to see it for herself, and decided she'd go downtown early the next morning.

Next, Maggie searched for news of Alma's nephew, Robert Winstead. One article came up. Clicking the link, she read of Robert's recent removal from the Town Council due to allegations of bribery. Maggie's first thought was that perhaps Robert had bribed someone so that they would choose his artist aunt for the downtown mural; but no, that wasn't it. Alma's nephew had been accused of attempting to bribe several of his fellow Council members into demolishing the old building on which the mural was painted. *Robert wanted the mural destroyed? Plus, he left Alma's urn behind. Definitely not a nice guy.*

Setting her laptop down on the dresser, Maggie tucked up in bed and set her phone alarm to wake her early in the morning. She wanted to get to the mural before sunrise.

***

It may have been a trick of the sunlight, but staring up at the mural, Maggie could almost see the farm laborers sweating. The sun on her own back felt warmer than it should for an early March day in North Carolina. It was as if she was right there with them, burning up in the sun.

She surveyed the two-story mural from edge-to-edge, then top-to-bottom. An artist herself, she recognized that this was a masterpiece: Alma's poignant masterpiece. The crop being harvested appeared to be jalapeño peppers, which surprised Maggie. Old farm paintings frequently depicted tobacco. The rear corner included a red barn, two paint horses — one brown and white, the other black and white — a man in a baseball cap with a cell phone to his ear. That's when Maggie realized it was a modern day farm scene, and the harvesters were migrant farm workers.

One of the farm workers nearest the front of the mural was wiping their arm across their brown forehead. Maggie felt sad as she imagined the hot sun beating down on the worker. It was a stunning piece of art, depicting contemporary farm workers in harsh conditions. Examining more details, she noted a fancy tractor, almost as tall as the barn. In the painting, it was half-hidden behind the horses and their fencing, unused.

Finally pulling herself away from the mural, Maggie drove the half-mile home. She parked in front of her house, sitting behind the wheel for several minutes, contemplating the sadness in the mural, before climbing from the car. As she locked the door, she made a snap decision and, instead of going into her home immediately, she walked down the sidewalk to The Coffee Haus. *If I'm going to use their WiFi, the least I can do is buy a coffee in support of them.*

She ended up buying a large coffee and a glistening pastry to take home. Settled at the kitchen table with her laptop, she connected to the WiFi again, then bit into the fruit-topped pastry. Brushing flakes and crumbles from the keys onto the kitchen table, she scanned her email. Nothing urgent, so she returned to her search for more about Alma Tyler.

She found a recent article on Alma's dear nephew's court appearance, and guessed that's why she'd been able to purchase the house at such a good price; he needed money. *Auntie Alma's property is funding his lawyer and he still left her ashes here*, she thought, shaking her head.

Popping the last bite of raspberry-and-phyllo into her mouth, Maggie cleaned the remaining crumbs from her laptop, the table, and shook phyllo bits from her shirt onto the floor. She swept the floor quickly and put away her laptop, then stared at the empty kitchen table.

"It's time to deal with that urn," she said aloud to the empty house. Pulling two paper towels from the roll, she set them in the center of the kitchen table. She turned the basement door key and headed down the stairs.

Crouching before Alma's urn, she said, "Your mural downtown is beautiful, Alma." She could have sworn the blue urn glowed for a moment. Glancing around the big room, she said, "I bet this was your art studio, Alma. I'm going to make it mine, too." Again, a blue brightness shone. That was when Maggie discovered the light source: a strong beam of sunlight streaming through the wide basement windows. "Natural light, even better for my studio."

Gently Maggie lifted the urn, pressing on the lid to hold it in place. She'd never actually touched an urn before and didn't know if it had a strong seal or not.

Stepping carefully, she mounted the stairs and placed the urn on the paper towels she'd laid out.

She opened the pantry door, where the Oreck was now hidden behind boxes labeled, *Art Supplies*. She found what she sought in the first box, a large paintbrush, and returned to the kitchen table. With a steady hand, she removed the dust from Alma's urn. "There, isn't that better?" The urn didn't respond, of course.

Placing two clean paper towels on the table, she lifted the urn from the dusty ones, then disposed of them. Her paintbrush, she washed thoroughly. While she didn't think it possible, she worried that some of the "dust" she'd removed might have been human ashes, and she didn't want to paint poor Alma onto her next canvas. She cringed at the thought as she dried the brush thoroughly.

Leaving the urn on the table, Maggie bustled around it, emptying the kitchen moving boxes. As she began stacking the empty boxes by the curb, a salt-and-pepper haired woman jogged over from a house across the street. "Are you throwing those boxes away? Could I have some? We're moving soon."

"Sure! I'm happy if you can make use of them. Do you want more? I have more inside." Maggie pulled the rest of the boxes outside and helped the woman carry them across to her porch. Once the boxes were stacked inside the neighbor's front door, they sat in the porch's rocking chairs and chatted for a bit. The woman, Danielle Meyer, excitedly described her upcoming move and her husband's recent retirement from the post office. Maggie shared a little about herself — living in an apartment, buying her first home, and finally making a living with her art — before turning the conversation to Alma Tyler.

"Oh, Alma was a character," Danielle said, pinching her chin and staring toward Maggie's house. "You know, she painted the *prettiest* pictures. And she was always so sweet to us. She brought us a homemade pumpkin pie every Halloween, and gave the *whole* neighborhood tomatoes from her garden in the summer. She was so sweet. She used to spend her

Christmases at the food pantry serving supper." Danielle laughed, "One year, she talked me into doing it with her. I was *never* so tired! I swear she was still going a mile a minute at the end of the night, even though she had 20 years on me!" Her face grew somber. "She died that next year and I never did it again."

Then, Maggie saw Danielle's face darken, and asked her what was wrong.

"Nothing's wrong, really. I was just thinking about that nephew of hers," she said, her nose wrinkling.

"From the face you made, I'm guessing you and your husband weren't close friends of Robert's."

Danielle waved with her hand, as if pushing that idea away. "Oh, hell no. We were glad to see the For Sale sign go up, even though we're leaving, too. He was *totally* the opposite of his auntie Alma, and I never thought he deserved to live in her house!"

"Wow, sounds like you had pretty strong feelings about him."

Danielle waved her hand again. "You might not know this, but he got charged with bribing people. Even before all that, he was an evil sum'bitch." She leaned away as if Maggie had been the one who swore, then whispered, "Excuse my language, but he was just a bad seed or something. The opposite of sweet Alma. I knew him in high school, back when he lived with his mama up on Railroad Street... she's dead now too. Back then, all of us girls knew to stay away from him. If there had been a *Me Too* movement then, let me tell you, he'd have been in jail a long time ago."

Maggie bit her tongue, then decided to tell the neighbor what she knew. "He left Alma's urn with her ashes in the basement. I found it the other day cleaning *behind the water heater*."

Danielle's light face went pure white. "Well that's just evil. I told you! Do you know when he moved out, he put a pile of her paintings out in the trash? He could have *sold* them, or given them away," she said, emphasized by a wave of both hands.

"Wow, I hope you saved them."

A devious smile spread across the woman's face.

Maggie joined her in a smile. "Good for you! Can I see them, Danielle?"

***

After showing Maggie the paintings, which were a series of local farm scapes, many showing similar themes to the mural with sweating farm hands or glass-encased tractors sitting idle. The last painting she showed Maggie depicted several dusty farm workers eating sandwiches seated under a tree, a long field stretching beyond them. As if inspired by the painting's subjects, Danielle said she needed to start making lunch for herself and her husband.

Maggie headed home, awed by Alma's use of color and light on the rescued canvases. No wonder the town had picked her to paint the mural.

As it was approaching noon, Maggie opened the refrigerator, scanning the sparse contents twice before grabbing a packet of cheese slices. She made two cheese sandwiches with her remaining bread, cut them into triangles, and opened a can of Dr. Pepper.

She ate ravenously, took a long drink from the soda can, and reached for the second sandwich. Her hand hovered above her paper plate as she discovered the second one wasn't there, but on another paper plate in front of Alma's urn.

"Good grief, Alma. Don't make me lose my mind." She snatched up the sandwich, threw away the urn's paper plate, and ate while pretending she hadn't just served lunch to a container of dead person.

***

Her brother Nicky showed up with his used washer and dryer — and a couple of his friends to move them — soon after lunch. "Wow, front loaders? These are awesome, brother. Thank you so much," she said, hugging Nicky.

While his friends hooked up the washer and dryer, Nicky joined Maggie in the kitchen. He pointed at the urn, one eyebrow raised. "You want to tell me what that thing is? And what is it doing on your kitchen table?"

She blushed. "I found it downstairs," she said.

"It's an urn." Her brother cocked an eyebrow at her.

"It is," she said, blushing again.

"It's on your *kitchen table*." He pointed at it again, as if stressing the point.

"Um," she said. "I wasn't sure what to do with it. It isn't empty..."

Nicky turned and stared at the urn. "So, you've got an urn full of somebody's ashes on--"

Maggie interrupted. "The name on it says it's Alma Tyler. She was a famous artist from town."

Her brother's head turned slowly from the urn to her. "It is ashes, sis. *Ashes*. On the table where you *eat*. Wouldn't it be better to throw it in the trash instead of letting it leak *where you eat*?"

"I don't think it can leak," she lied, avoiding a direct response to his question.

Nicky gaped at her, then shook his head. "Well, I hope you throw it away. Gross." He walked to the basement door and, as he descended the steps, she heard him mutter, "I won't be eating here any time soon."

***

Half an hour later, Nicky yelled up the stairs, "Everything's hooked up!"

She thanked her brother and his friends profusely as she walked them out. When her brother glanced back toward the kitchen, she again thanked him for giving her his old washer and dryer. "I really needed them, Nicky. Thank you so much."

He gave her a squeeze, then left with his helpers without saying another word.

She closed the front door, locked it, and leaned her back against it. Before anyone else came to visit, she needed to find a more permanent place for Alma Tyler's ashes. Neither the ashes, nor the urn, would be going in the trash.

***

Maggie dreamed of Alma for the second time that night. The dust — ashes — took form, and old Alma's face appeared on the silhouette. She gave Maggie the same nose tweak, and laughed the same laugh, but Maggie continued sleeping and dreaming.

Alma talked to Maggie about her life as an artist, and how pleased she was to have another artist take up residence. In her dream, Maggie told Alma how much she loved the life shown within the mural, and the mural's poignant message about the harshness of farm work, even in the new millennium. "I can't understand your nephew wanting to destroy such a work of art."

Alma shrugged sadly, sending ash swirling round her head. "My grandfather fell in love with my grandmother when he saw her working the farm; they married less than a month later. They moved away to raise their children, and my father told me it was because of how his family had treated Grampa for marrying Grandma."

"Oh, Alma, that's awful." Maggie said, tearing up while dreaming.

Alma sighed. "When I moved back here to set up my studio, I saw immediately what my Dad had meant. Robert talked down to me worse than anyone... and he talked down to everyone I ever saw him interact with. That's why in my mural I included Robert yacking on a cell phone instead of working."

Maggie hugged Alma, who squeezed her in return, and Maggie awoke.

***

After that, every week or so, Maggie dreamt of the artist — not so often as she'd lose her mind, but often enough to enjoy the chats with Alma. She began to think of the dreams as art lessons, ignoring the fact that her teacher had been dead for years.

In dreams, the two artists conversed about arts, brush choices, inspiration, and the state of the world. Alma shared her secrets for working with paints. She explained how she created the "sweating" effect within the downtown mural using a custom paint mix with flakes of mica.

Maggie listened and learned. She remembered more than she usually did of her dreams. She followed Alma's guidance, and more of Maggie's paintings sold — faster than they had been selling. She knew her skills were improving, thanks to Alma.

***

The first week of April, Maggie yielded to the call of the sunshine. She wanted new subjects to paint, as interest in her art was expanding. The Raleigh gallery which normally sold her paintings, and the Hope Wells gallery which had recently offered her a small display space, were both pressing her to provide pieces. She grabbed two sketchbooks, her favorite graphite pencils, a jacket as an afterthought, and scooped up her keys.

She started driving — windows down — through downtown. Passing Alma's mural, she felt the urge to venture into the farmlands it depicted. She turned around by taking several lefts along side streets, then a right onto the two-lane road that led beyond the town limits toward the next town. There would be plenty of farms out this way. Depending on the planned crops, some farms might be plowing or planting already. It being a Tuesday, a workday afternoon, she hoped she'd see some farm or someone to sketch.

When Maggie reached the next town with no luck, she turned around and headed back to Hope Wells and home. Despite the sunshine and warm weather, none of the fields she'd passed had activity.

She made one stop on the way home. There, she pulled to the side of the road and sketched an interesting, broad tree surrounded on two sides by tombstones. No one from the nearby house came out to complain, and she completed her sketch undisturbed.

Returning home, she laid her sketches and materials on the kitchen counter and rummaged through the refrigerator for something to eat. Cheese sandwiches were fast and easy, and after she'd wolfed them down, she grabbed a glass of ice water and headed downstairs with the new sketch.

The worked on the canvas the rest of the afternoon, and several afternoons following, during the hours when natural light permeated the basement. She used the basement's overhead lights while she worked in her studio, but preferred the hues the sunlight brought inside with it during the day.

By Friday at sunset, she called the painting done. The tree on the canvas sparkled in sunlight, its branches bearing the small leaves of Spring. Below the branches where the tombstones had stood, she'd painted only luminous grasses. She didn't want death overshadowing the beauty and light of the tree as she'd seen it on that sunny afternoon. While she was mostly happy with her creation, she had a nagging feeling that something was missing. Calling it a night, she decided to drive by the tree again before finishing and signing the canvas.

Alma visited her in her dream that night. The artist said that she was right to consider the painting unfinished. "While it is beautiful, Maggie, it is most certainly missing something, and it isn't tombstones."

Waking early on Saturday morning, Maggie paced. She was eager to take a drive to see the tree again, but made herself wait until the sun climbed higher in the sky. She ate an early lunch with one eye on the clock, which seemed to her to be moving slower than usual.

Finally, the clock showed 12:30pm and she could wait no longer. She bounded from the house, then ran back inside for her sketchbooks and pencils, then locked the door and hustled to the car.

In ten minutes, she was parked on the side of the road. The tree was washed in sunlight as it had been on her previous visit. She took a few photos with her cell phone; no need for another sketch at this point.

Seeing motion through the lens, she lowered the phone and saw two men approaching the tree. They reached it and she could see clearly it was an elderly white man wearing overalls, and a teenager with dark skin and wavy black hair. *Maybe his grandson?*

Maggie approached and asked their permission for her to sketch them. The old man introduced himself as Bud

Ashford, the teen as his grandson Ernie, and asked who she was. When she introduced herself and explained her plan to create a painting of the tree, he laughed. "Taking after Alma Tyler, are you? Alma was an artist, kind of famous around here, and she sketched Ernie, his mama, and me back when Ern was barely walking. We ended up in one of her pretty pictures."

"That's wonderful!" Maggie made a mental note to look online for Alma's painting of them. Carefully she wrote down their names, asking for spellings of each. She sketched the men from back by the road, as they hung a swing from one of the tree's thick branches.

As if on cue, as the two finished securing the second rope to the swing, a small child ran over from a nearby house and straight to them. The child was on the swing a second later and pumping their legs, increasing the arc until they were swooping ten feet in the air in both directions.

Maggie moved closer and finished her sketch of the swing now attached to the tree. Then, she turned a page and began sketching the older man's lined face as he beamed at the child. "This is my grand-baby Linda," the man said to her.

Before leaving, she sketched the teenager's face and the child's, then snapped photos of them all — catching the little girl at the zenith of her swinging — and thanked them for letting her be a part of their day.

***

When she finished adding the tree-swing and girl to her tree painting, Maggie pronounced it finished and signed her name. She decided that, since the family depicted lived so close to town, she would send this painting off to the Raleigh gallery.

It sold in two days.

By then, Maggie had painted portraits of the old man with his grandson, and a smaller painting of the tree alone. The latter, she sent to the local gallery, where it sold two weeks later.

Inspired, she began driving around the area on weekends, sketching farm families at work and play. By the end of summer, she'd begun venturing to neighboring counties and produced dozens of paintings depicting farm life.

Alma encouraged Maggie in her dreams. "I believe you've found your niche, young lady." Alma explained that, as her grandmother had been a migrant worker from South America, Alma had been drawn to the farm workers. With her portrayals of their struggles, Alma had drawn a national following. "You are drawn to the farmers and their families, and your paintings show the hard labor of farmers of all colors. Capturing their contemporary struggles may lead you to many admirers, and historical significance."

Maggie had dismissed this idea when Alma offered it. She couldn't imagine a following beyond the two North Carolina galleries that were selling her works. And historical? *No way am I that good of an artist*, she thought. It shocked Maggie when, on a Saturday soon after, she ventured several counties away and — upon stopping to sketch a picnicking family — was asked by the farmer's wife if, "you'll be making us as famous as old Bud Ashford."

The idea that she might just be painting "history" shook Maggie to the core. After much thinking, and dream conversations, she determined to do the best captures of farm life as realistically as she could.

***

That evening as Maggie dreamed, Alma reached out and honked her nose again.

"Why do you do that?" Maggie asked. She didn't mind it anymore, but even after all the conversation they'd shared, she didn't understand it.

Alma smiled. "I was an only child. My father used to tweak my nose. He didn't hug, but he'd tweak my nose as a way of comforting me. Our farm was a fun place to be, my father kind — mother, too, but she hugged. When I had friends come over after school, my dad would pass out snacks. Nothing fancy, mind you, just apples or boiled cabbage, or other things from our farm that he could afford to share. If he notice one of my friends was down-in-the-mouth... they didn't all have good homes, nor necessarily enough food... my father would tweak their nose, too, to cheer them up. So, I'm trying to cheer you, young lady." She shrugged, still smiling.

Maggie smiled back. "That's sweet, Alma. I guess I don't mind it now."

***

At the end of the month, Maggie sat down with her bills spread out on the kitchen table. Using her laptop, she paid several online, then wrote checks for the last two, and gleefully read her remaining balance. Her checking account still held $2,015.45 and everything was paid for the month.

Sure, she'd been making a living for some time now, but before she'd bought the house her rent had taken more of her earnings, and at that time she hadn't been selling as many pieces. Having $100 for a month of food and gas had been her norm, and she'd eaten many a sandwich to save money.

Now, she felt as if she had succeeded! Finding her niche, with Alma's encouragement, had changed everything. She could buy a fancy cup of coffee, burn gas on country drives and refill the car's gas tank, and not overdraw her account. If she kept it up, she could save for rainy, no-sales months, and be comfortable for however long interest in her niche would last. She made a mental note to keep her mind open for a new niche, should it become necessary.

Daydreams of future sales swept through her mind. If sales kept going for the next six months, she might buy a new car, or if people kept buying her art, she might pay off the mortgage ten years early. When her imagining reached creation of a custom van with an art studio inside it for painting at the side of the country roads, she shook her head and brought herself back to reality.

Walking the two enveloped checks to the mailbox, she flipped up the flag, checked out the stars above as she breathed in the salty night air, and returned to the house.

She climbed the stairs and prepared for, then climbed into, bed. Surprisingly, Alma visited her in her dreams that night, much sooner than the every-two-weeks pattern to which she'd become accustomed. Alma patted her arm and said, "Do you know how lucky you are to be successful in your dream job? How few people get to do what they love every day?"

"Yes, of course," Maggie responded. "I'm doing well with my painting, and thank you for helping me reach this point."

"You've done that yourself, my girl, and it is good," Alma said. "Remember that. Paying the bills is good. Wishing for luxuries is nice, but they are not necessary to be happy. Yes, you may wish for more money, but money is a means to happiness, not happiness itself. Let it sit in the bank, where it will grow and shrink, and paint to your heart's content."

"I will. I promise."

Alma patted her arm. "Promise yourself, not me." The artist's spirit added, "I'm proud of you, Maggie."

***

Two months after moving into the house, Maggie stood at her easel happily applying paint to her latest canvas. Sun streamed through the basement window facing the back yard. Alma's urn caught the sunlight from its perch on a tall, blue table Maggie had made specifically as an urn pedestal.

"What do you think of this one? I think it's one of my best ever." She looked at the urn, expecting no reply and receiving none. That was fine. Maggie would show the painting to Alma during their next ethereal lesson.

Maggie shuffled through the sketches she'd made, the basis of the almost-finished painting on her easel. She'd visited one of the working farms outside of town the past three mornings. After getting permission from those working the field, she'd sketched several of the older workers, which included farmer Bud and his teen grandson. She'd started to sketch a 14-year-old among those working with Bud, but the young woman's eyes — full of sadness — had broken Maggie's heart and she couldn't finish the sketch. The rest of her time she'd focused on sketching the laborers who looked to be older than herself. She could bear that tired look more in the older people than she could in those who had a long life ahead of them.

When she'd returned with her sketches this morning, she'd made a decision to give a portion of the proceeds from her art sales to a nonprofit supporting the younger farm workers. Somehow, she'd help them to have choices in their lives, an option other than toiling in the fields for low wages. Maybe in a way she could help the generations of farmers to come, too.

Noticing a detail she'd missed, she reached for her brush. A few more strokes, and she believed this painting would be done. By next week, she could send it to a gallery to sell.

Hearing a barely-audible knock from upstairs, Maggie cocked her head and listened. There it was again. Someone was at her front door. She set down the brush. "I'll be back, Alma," she said as she sprinted up the stairs.

Peeking through the side-window curtain, Nicky and Margo were standing at her front door. Maggie swung the door wide. She wore a large, welcoming grin on her face as she invited them in; though she steeled herself for a goodness-knows-why-they-are-here visit. It was a weekday, and Margo rarely ventured from her routine — which literally listed "Family Visit" as a Saturday option.

She led her siblings into the living room. "Would either of you like coffee?"

Both shook their heads. "No thank you," Margo said, and she nudged Nicky.

Here it comes, Maggie thought.

"We're worried about you, Maggie," Nicky said.

"Me? Why? What have I done to cause you to worry... and show up on my doorstep on a work day?"

"It's your paintings, sis," Margo said. "What happened to all your beautiful landscapes? The old barns and pretty buildings. Those were selling just fine. Why did you switch to these... other subjects?"

Maggie didn't answer her question. Instead, she said, "I don't understand what your problem is. I'm selling more canvases than ever. Why aren't you guys happy for me?"

Margo gaped at her. "Are you kidding me, Mags? Your new stuff is probably selling to ghouls. Who else would want your... the... grotesque... paintings of *poor* people."

That was it, then. Margo with the perfect husband, perfect house, and perfect kids didn't like seeing images of poor farmers and their struggles. Anger stirring, Maggie turned on her sister. "Well, I'm sorry if it offends your sensibilities." She turned viciously toward Nicky. One of the better brothers, yet here he stood beside Margo. "How about you, Nicky? Too horrifying to see hard-working people represented? You want me painting barns with dainty women lying in the hay? Happy industrial farmers in million dollar tractors?"

Nicky help up both hands in front of him defensively. "Margo's worried about you. I'm just here to keep the peace."

At that, Margo gaped at him. "Seriously, Nicky? You keep joking about her keeping a dead body on her kitchen table, telling us all we shouldn't come here to eat? *And* all the way here you were complaining about how awful it is that her horrid paintings are selling. Now you want to play the good guy?"

"*You* said that, not me. I just agreed with you so you'd shut up," Nicky protested.

Maggie thought he sounded genuine, but noticed he didn't respond to the dead-body-jokes accusation. Now she understood why none of her siblings had come for dinner any of the times she'd invited them.

She'd had enough. "I think you both better go," Maggie said flatly. She turned from them and marched to the front door. Swinging it wide, she waved with her arm toward the opening, indicating they leave her house. Thankfully, they complied without another word.

Maggie stood in the doorway and watched them climb into Nicky's car and drive away. For a moment, she thought about visiting Danielle across the street again; then remembered the moving truck had come a week ago. Danielle and her family were off to somewhere new, and there would be no more chats. On moving day, Maggie had let Danielle pick one of her paintings to take with her. The "grotesque" subjects hadn't put off Danielle; in fact, she'd taken a long time to choose one, as she'd liked several "very much." Danielle's choice had borne the image of a light-haired woman with her hair tied up, picked green beans piled in her skirt, which Danielle had said reminded her of her grandmother.

"Grotesque, indeed," Maggie mumbled as she slammed and locked the door.

"Can you believe the nerve of them," she said as she returned to the basement art studio. She shook her head toward Alma's urn, the sunlight choosing that moment to make its blue sheen glow. "I know, right?" she said, as if the urn had spoken. "And you haven't been in the kitchen since that *one day*, for heaven's sake!" She picked up a brush, surveyed the current canvas, and dipped into a deep brown pool of paint. Wiping the brush gently, she began applying a freckle on the farmer's visage before her. "How dare they call you grotesque, Bud. You're amazing."

***

That evening after washing splotches of paint from her hair and arms — she'd had a successful day and finished two paintings — Maggie settled into bed. It was about time for her to again dream of Alma; she was eager to get to sleep.

As soon as she dozed, Alma appeared and Maggie relayed her conversation with her siblings.

"Family can do more harm than strangers," Alma told her in the dream. "You've met my nephew." Alma laughed, a strangled, angry sound. "Then again, if it weren't for Robert's neglect, I wouldn't be here with you, my artist friend."

"You understand. And you're a wonderful teacher! My work is so much better now. I'm grateful for your being here with me... in some form." Maggie excitedly showed the older woman her latest works. "My paintings are selling much faster now, and I don't think that would be true without you teaching me, Alma."

"I enjoy our time together, Maggie. You're a good student." Alma's wispy hand reached out and tweaked her nose.

Maggie smiled in her sleep, as her next art lesson began.

A Trick of the Memory

I can feel it, she thought. *This is different.*

Family and friends had chastised her when, in her younger years, she'd said that she had a poor memory. She was making a self-fulfilling prophecy, they had told her. So, she had taken pains to think of her memory as a good one.

Everyone forgets why they went into a room, at some point, she knew. *That* was normal. So, *this* must be fine.

I have a good memory, she told herself.

Yes, her memory had been imperfect even when she was young; but *this* in recent months was different and she knew it. She didn't want to know it. *This* wasn't walking into a room and forgetting why she was there. *This* had expanded to the point that it frightened her. *This* was not just forgetting now, but forgetting that she'd forgotten. Or worse, *remembering*, with a wave of fear, that she'd done so.

This was having to navigate home from the grocery store so she wouldn't miss her home exit. Again. *This* was becoming confused and thinking she'd made a wrong turn because none of the houses or farm fields looked familiar; and then rounding a corner to find her street looming ahead. Familiar places — she'd driven by thousands of times — weren't familiar every time. Not anymore.

This was setting two alarms, minutes apart, to ensure she didn't forget to give the cat its morning medicine after turning off the first alarm. *This* was sitting down at the computer instead of walking into the kitchen to give the cat its medicine. *This* was, mid-day, *Did I give the cat its medicine this morning?* How could she have forgotten to give the cat its medicine when she'd set two alarms to remind her, and would have had to turn them off when the annoying sounds burst forth from her cell phone? *Did I set alarms for today?*

Is there any evidence that I gave the cat its medicine? Yes! A crumb of the cheddar cheese used to encase the pill is on the counter. *It's still soft.* The cat *must* have been given its medicine because she'd cleaned the counter that morning while the coffee brewed.

Had she cleaned it *today*? Was it this morning when she wiped down the counter so thoroughly? That's the way she remembered it. Except, how would she know if she'd forgotten, if she'd forgotten that she'd forgotten?

This was different.

Seeing the clock and realizing it was lunchtime, she opened the dishwasher to grab a plate, and a smell assailed her. *What could possibly be in there to stink like that?* Dirty dishes were piled within, neatly but filled. *When did the dishwasher last run? It must be run now! Pour in the liquid. Close the door. Wait, turn it on and then close the door. There, now the dishes are being cleaned. Good.*

When did I last eat? She looked at the clock and saw it was lunchtime.

She'd recently developed a new habit: each time she prepared something to eat, she forced herself to think. *What did I eat today?* Remembering what meals or snacks she'd eaten had become important for some reason. To eat some new thing, she pressed herself to remember what she'd eaten all day to that point. She couldn't always remember. Peering into the trash, she sought evidence to spur her memory. Once she could recall her previous meals, then she'd proceed: preparing a plate, sitting down, eating, cleaning up; only to wonder, hours later, what she had eaten.

This was different.

Had she washed her hands before she ate? Why was she wondering that? Of course, she washed her hands before she made lunch! She washed her hands all the time. A faint memory tickled at her brain, one in which she recalled noticing dirt under her fingernails while holding a sandwich. *Could that memory be real? I would not have taken a bite if I'd seen such a gross thing.* Yet she remembered the taste of peanut butter and jelly — what kind of jelly wasn't part of the memory. That fragment was gone.

How many fragments are gone?

Don't think about that, she urged herself. *It's a question with no reliable answer.* How could she know what she doesn't know? *Don't think about how many fragments are gone, or how many memories were lost. It's too scary.*

Sitting down in front of her computer, she opened her email program. *Goodness, that's more emails than usual.* She stared at the Inbox. She expected the emails to be all from today; but there were three-days-worth of new ones. *Haven't I checked my email every day? I work at the computer every day, don't I? Didn't I?* She checked the Sent folder to see what was sent the day before. Nothing. Nothing sent since Tuesday. *How could I have forgotten to work for three days?*

This is too frightening to think about, too fragmented. *I have a good memory. I have a good memory!* She repeated the thought over and over.

Was this her self-fulfilled prophecy? She couldn't have brought this on herself, could she? *Perhaps this is a gift from God.*

All those times the painful memories had surfaced, and she had begged God to take them away, to stop her from thinking of the times of sickness, of death, and of despair. *Take that memory away, please, Lord*, she had implored hundreds of times over the years, if not thousands.

Maybe this was His gift to her. Only, the memories she'd begged be taken away had taken others with them — along with her ability to remember for a few seconds, "Give the cat its medicine," when the alarms went off.

Perhaps God was a little bit like a genie, playing games with wishes for a chuckle. "You should have been more specific."

Perhaps she should have been.

Growing Old

Owen Bannerman slammed the can of baked beans on the kitchen counter. The already cracked surface gained a new flaw, a small piece breaking loose and skittering across the counter into a nook behind the flour canister.

Owen cursed the can opener, the can of beans, the counter, and lastly screamed at his hands for being weak. He violently rummaged through the kitchen cabinets. If he could no longer operate the can opener, he was going to have to relent and set up the electric one. That felt like failure to him.

Angry as he was at his hands, he ignored their sharp twangs when, finally locating the electric can opener, he snatched at it and cut both index fingers. He left them bleeding as punishment as he plugged in the hated device and forced the can onto it. After a brief whirring, the lid clicked, and he grabbed the can. The beans splashed as he dumped them into the waiting bowl.

As the bowl spun in the microwave, Owen washed the blood from his fingers. Small cuts, barely needing bandaging, but he stuck two small strip bandages on the nicks so he wouldn't have to look at them, and so that he could eat his beans without dripping blood into them. If there was one thing he didn't want in his food, it was his blood.

Owen's capitulation to the electric device was one in a list of his failures. He ticked them off in his mind as he ate spoonfuls of his hot lunch. Driver's license gone. Car sold. Bus pass purchased. That last had been his biggest failure, in his mind. He hated the bus... always had.

Before he'd become unable to drive, he'd become unable to open jars. The day he'd dropped the jar of pickles, then cut his big toe on a piece of glass he had missed, had been a turning point. It was a failure with a capital F.

Soon after, he'd needed to hire a housekeeper — no longer able to hold the broom or push the vacuum without his hands turning in on themselves and attempting to stay there, claw-like. At least the cleaner was cheap. She didn't talk much, either, which he appreciated.

Sure, he was lonely and he knew it. None of his nieces and nephews, nor his also-aging siblings, had visited him in years. He liked that, just as he did the housekeeper's silence. Silence all the time shouldn't have been all right, but it was fine with him. He enjoyed the ache of loneliness; reveled in the agony.

He scooped at his bowl and discovered the beans were gone. For a moment, he stared, mouth aghast at the realization that he'd eaten his whole lunch while lost in thought. Smacking his lips, he could still taste them, and wanted more. Angry at the beans' inability to satisfy him, he dropped the bowl in the sink and walked outside.

Lowering himself onto a lounge chair on the back patio, Owen listened to the birds and let his thoughts go. He closed his eyes and turned up his chin, allowing the sun to warm his skin. He heard the birds chirping and tweeting in all directions and focused on their sounds.

His legs, jutting down the long chair, began to ache. He shifted, and his hip joined the achy party.

In the old days, back when he was twenty, even thirty, he'd had the same aches. He knew that they weren't pain, but motivators. Back then, they had motivated him to get up, go out, do things, meet people. When he'd obeyed their egging on, he would be allowed to relax at night and sleep. The aches would leave him alone for a while.

When they returned each time, he knew what to do and did it, temporarily enjoying the calm that followed.

Since he'd reached the age of sixty, he'd discovered he could no longer get out, do things, meet people, and placate the ache enough to reach the calm after-times. Since the day he'd dropped the infernal, stuck-shut pickle jar, he'd found he grew tired after taking a shower and getting dressed. He rose to meet no motivations.

He had tried to press on, at first. Sixty wasn't that old, he knew. He'd fought his body and done all that he could, resting when he needed to rest, the ache never leaving him. Once, he'd managed to get out, had taken *that woman* out for the evening, but his body had felt downright frail, his need for rests frequent, and when he finally returned home, sleep wouldn't come. The ache hadn't stopped as expected and hadn't stopped since.

Behind him, he heard the front door squeak open, and the housekeeper yelled, "Hello, Mr. Bannerman! It's Wendy!"

A part of him was glad she'd said her name. He could never remember it. "I'm outside, Wendy," he said in a sweet voice. He'd always talked sweet to women. Just because he was an angry old man, his body weak now, didn't mean he'd lost his manners.

He tried to recall what he had been thinking about before he heard Wendy coming in the door? Unable to remember, he focused again on the bird songs.

***

Some minutes later, his train of thought returned. He'd been thinking about *that woman*. Yes, it had been the day after taking her out that he'd admitted that he'd reached a new low.

Well, really if he admitted it to himself, it was after he'd read the morning newspaper the morning before he'd seen *that woman*. Hidden deep within its finger-inking pages, there had been a notice that his dear friend, Detective Anthony Stewart, had retired. A slow news day, apparently, as the article ran several columns and included a photo of no-longer-a-Detective Stewart beaming, surrounded by various other detectives Owen didn't recognize.

Time had passed and his dear friend was no longer chasing the bad guys.

No longer chasing me.

Why run if no one is chasing?

His decision to take that woman out later that evening had been a reaction, perhaps motivated by a ridiculous hope that the detective might un-retire if he resurfaced.

Instead, his body had forced him into retirement by refusing to let him rest after the grueling night. His body had put on the brakes; he could no longer placate the aching within him. If he'd had any bit of self-respect, he might have continued to fight against the feelings of uselessness. Instead, he had given in. Owen's remaining desire to press on disappeared. There was no point. Why continue on if nobody cares anymore?

***

Detective Stewart had come into Owen's life during his late twenties. Owen had immediately adored the tenacious detective. His thrill had increased in his mid-forties when Detective Stewart had almost tracked him down. "Almost only counts in horseshoes and hand grenades," Owen had taunted the detective in a carefully worded, handled-with-gloves letter. In the decades that followed, Owen had frequently taunted Detective Stewart — who had never come close again.

On the day that Owen had read of Stewart's retirement, he'd given it one more go, failed, and shut down. He'd found not relief, but frustration added to the constant ache. How could the chaser stop chasing and call the race ended? They hadn't reached the finish line.

***

Owen's thoughts were disrupted by the arrival of Wendy beside his lounge chair. Shielding his eyes as he looked up at her, he saw that she was holding out the morning newspaper. "I thought you might want this while you relax out here," she said, before setting it in his raised hand and retreating into the house.

He heard the vacuum start as he turned from the front page to the inside pages. Rolling his eyes, he focused on the small text and continued scanning the day's boring-to-him news. On page 6, he perked up, even smiled, when he found a follow-up story on *that woman's* disappearance. As he read the quote from a source at the police department, he chuckled at what he perceived as incompetence. *What kind of idiot tells a reporter that they have no leads on a murder?*

Well, no one would ever find him, nor *that woman*, now that Stewart was a regular citizen. No young detectives could be a match for himself, Owen believed. He'd out-matched Stewart for decades, after all.

Stewart's old cases would be in a box somewhere waiting for someone to get around to them. Whomever replaced Stewart wouldn't even know where to start and would likely stick to reacting as new cases hit his desk. Or hers, Owen thought and laughed aloud. Women weren't supposed to be detectives in Owen's mind. They were for... his thoughts turned sad at realizing he would never do anything he wanted to do to a woman again. His anger returned.

He crushed the newspaper and creaked upward from the chair. Storming into the house — as much as he was able to storm these days — he threw it onto the counter. Wendy, who was wiping down the counters, said nothing. That was good. He didn't want to hear a damn word.

Making the long climb upstairs to the bathroom, Owen sat on the edge of the tub. He wished for his body to give up the ghost. If he didn't have to run, he may as well be dead.

***

A sound startled him from his thoughts. It had been the doorbell, and in quick succession it rang again. He heard Wendy's footsteps creaking on the downstairs hall floorboards. He pricked up his ears as the door creaked open, and Wendy's muffled voice was joined by another woman's. Leaning forward, head tilted, he tried to catch the conversation but understood no words. He rose from the tub edge with an angry grunt and swung the bathroom door wide. It was his house, damn it, and if he wanted to know what was being talked about, he would damn well go to the front door.

A young woman in a nicely fitting suit stood in the foyer speaking with the house cleaner. She and Wendy looked up at him as he descended the stairs much faster than he had in months.

"Well, hello," he said sweetly. "I'm Owen Bannerman. Are you here to see me or are you selling something?"

The young woman in the suit smiled brightly, but her eyes did not reflect the smile. As he reached the bottom of the stairs, puzzled, he asked, "Can I help you?"

The woman nodded to Wendy, who stepped outside, replaced rapidly by two uniformed police officers. "Yes, Owen

Bannerman, you can definitely help me," the woman said. She flashed a badge, followed by one of the uniformed officers beginning the as-seen-on-television Miranda rights as his mate handcuffed Owen.

Without a word, Owen allowed himself to be led outside. Ahead of him, next to a patrol car parked in the driveway stood no-longer-a-Detective Stewart.

"Now I can retire for real," Stewart said to the suited young woman as Owen was pressed into the back of a nearby police cruiser. "You were right about my needing a fresh pair of eyes. Sorry I put you off for so long."

"Couldn't have done it without your careful notes down the years. Team effort."

Stewart chortled, "The video of him on the bus with blood on his shoes sure helped."

Wendy stood silently, wringing her hands, before she said, "I always knew there was something off about that man."

After All The Waiting

She drove carefully at the speed limit, fighting the urge to drive faster as she approached her destination. A visit that she had thought would only take place in her head, a shameful act against her usual kind nature, she now looked forward to putting her thoughts into action.

She couldn't believe her luck: having a client meeting so close by. Living a thousand miles away from the graveyard, she hadn't planned to ever *really* go. It was one thing to be joyful; yet another to fly across the country to celebrate in-person on the grave. Sure, she could be petty sometimes, but making a special trip of it? That would have been far beyond petty, possibly immoral.

Instead, the schedule had worked perfectly. She'd finished her client meeting, and had hours before her red-eye flight.

The sun was setting as she gently rolled the steering wheel of the rental car to the right, the car turning onto a strip of dark asphalt and motoring up the long drive to the hilltop church. Grave markers of varying sizes dotted the landscape surrounding the medieval-looking structure of stone and stained glass.

She parked at the far edge of the church's parking lot. Grabbing the flowers on the seat beside her, she stepped out, locked the car, and made a beeline for the grave she sought — its location confirmed in-advance using the cemetery's online records.

After a few false starts, she sorted out the geography and found the grave. Seeing the small tombstone, the name of her tormentor engraved in neat block letters, her anger rose. Images flashed across her mind... mere highlights to the years of torment this woman had inflicted. It didn't matter, in that moment, that the torments were decades behind her, and in truth had only swallowed up three years of her life.

It had been the longest three years. The dead woman had been her manager at her first job, and the way the manager had treated the workers had created what was referred to these days as a *hostile work environment*. It had been a time of dreaded weekdays, and frequent demeaning — to herself and others.

No more, she thought, and smirked.

Placing a flower from the store-bought bouquet onto each of the surrounding graves, as a peace offering in her mind, she returned to the headstone she'd come to see. No flowers here; that did not surprise her.

Bitch.

She stepped onto the grass-less soil in front of the small gravestone and began. First, she danced a jig, hearing a raucous violin in her head. Then, she moved on to the cabbage patch dance, thrusting her arms to the side and across jubilantly many times, before twirling on the grave.

In mid twirl, she heard a throat clearing. She stopped and was horrified to find herself facing a man in a long robe and white collar. *The church's priest!* She gasped, her cheeks reddening.

The man in the collar tilted his head, shooting her a look she didn't understand. He said, "All my years here at this church, my time spent in this cemetery, and I'd never seen people dancing on graves until now."

"I'm sorry, Father," she flushed crimson, shame rising, and bowed her head.

He held up his hand. "I said *until now*. These past few weeks, since this woman," he nodded toward the small headstone, "was laid to rest, there have been many visitors to this grave. The first visitor I caught dancing, I admonished. After speaking with the third and fourth, dancing together, I began to understand." He sighed a deep, heaving sigh.

"I've lost count, now. You may be the tenth or the fifteenth such capering visitor. I don't know how I feel about it from a scriptural viewpoint, but I've begun to think it is the grave's occupant who may be most deserving of my admonishment."

She flushed again, but less so.

The priest chuckled, peering at her with a mischeviousness twist at the corner of his mouth. "I'm beginning to think I need to have the ground reconsecrated. Grass seed won't even sprout here."

She said nothing, only nodding.

He sighed again, but with a smile for her. "I'll leave you to it, and to your... joy. I do have one request, though. I'll be starting a service in an hour, and I would appreciate if you're done before my parishioners begin to arrive."

She nodded again. "I will be. Thank you, Father."

When he was sufficiently far away, she began her jig again, listening to the vibrant notes in her head as her feet stomped the footprint-graven ground.

The Camouflaged Woman

I knew her as Violet Skye. Understanding that she'd chosen that name for herself, I found it absurdly attention-grabbing. For someone with a woeful tale of relocation, hiding, and identity changes, she'd sure picked a name that shone a spotlight on her. I didn't tell her that I thought the name she'd chosen seemed the opposite of camouflage.

Violet was about my age, mid-twenties at most. She shared with me that she had spent the past five years of her life renting with cash and staying under the radar. She didn't own a car, and she'd applied for the job at the warehouse because she figured that few people would see her amongst the boxes and pallets.

Her covert living wasn't the only odd thing about her, either. Violet had powers of persuasion — never used them on me. I don't mean she could talk people into things; I mean, she could *compel* people to do what she wanted and they were *unable to resist*. Some kind of mind thing. I don't know what to call it.

Violet admitted to me that she knew it was wrong to use her powers against people, but she justified it as a "sometimes necessary part of survival." I was happy that she respected me enough not to use it to push me around. She said that she loved that she could tell me her secrets and trust me to keep quiet.

Said I was the first and only person she trusted, and the first she'd considered a friend. I'm just me, just an ordinary person, so I don't know why that is. Sure, more than once I wondered if she'd *persuaded* me into keeping her secret. There was precedent, I knew, from her stories of persuading others without their knowledge.

One such story was from just before she came to work at the warehouse. When her boyfriend was mugged and ended up in the hospital, she walked the block where it had happened. She went back each night until she found a man who looked like the police sketch made from her boyfriend's description. She'd urged the man to confess — a true confession, she didn't persuade an innocent man. Within an hour of her finding him, the mugger had turned himself in to the police. I know it was under her extreme suggestion because Violet told me that herself. The day he was in the papers, that's when she told me all about it. I think it was her first or second week here at the warehouse.

She never told her boyfriend what she'd done for him; never told him about her powers, at all. Unlike me, he didn't even know her real name! When she broke up with him, she said she persuaded him to forget her. I found that fascinating!

It took her a while to get over him, she admitted, wishing she could make herself forget like she did "as a favor to him." Eventually, she stopped talking about him.

She found a rebound boyfriend, and seemed to be happy. He doesn't know her real name or powers, either.

***

But, let me start her story back a little further with Violet's mother; that's where the name changing started. This is all straight from the horse's mouth. Violet's adoptive mother had named her Stephanie Kingman as a baby. Before her adoption, her birth name was Jennifer Marley. She hadn't especially liked either of the names given to her, not firsts nor lasts. Before her mother died, she confessed that the adoption hadn't been legal. Not wanting her adopted daughter taken away, her mother had changed their names and moved often.

Violet told me that when her mother explained their many names and frequent moving — Violet had lived in ten different states as a child — her life began to make sense. Until that point, my friend thought name changing was just what someone did when they moved!

Violet told me she'd kind of liked that her mother let her pick her own names once she was old enough. Start over brand new and get to call yourself whatever you wanted? Who wouldn't like to do that?

When her mother passed away, she went on the road. She said back then she worried that whatever had been chasing her mother might be coming, though at that point Stephanie was eighteen and doubted anybody would be coming to claim her and undo the adoption. But she ran. "Best to move on than find out," was the way she put it.

Her first job was at a grocery store, and she used her latest name, Stephanie Marks, and her Stephanie Kingman Social Security number. It was the only number that she had. When bills from the funeral home found her a year later, she skipped again, ditching all names and numbers connected with her mother.

She said that she'd learned quickly what *not* to do. Violet followed her mother's lead with frequent hair-dying and weight changes to disguise herself. Once she mentioned to me that she gained twenty pounds on purpose so her face would change, and no one she'd known would recognize her. As skinny as Violet was, I knew that had been for a previous identity. How many identities she used, I can't say.

Like I said, I met her when she came to work at the warehouse; I was already working there. That's when she gave herself the name, Violet Skye. I don't know how she got that past the people in Human Resources, what with a made-up Social Security number and such a unique chosen name, but I know that while she worked here, she persuaded the boss to cash her checks for her each payday. Banks must be harder to get past, I guess.

When she told me about her made up names, I wondered if her desire to be seen — as we all wish when we're young adults — led to her chosen identity. A name like *Violet Skye* doesn't blend in, in my opinion. It sticks in people's memories. Not to mention, the streak of purple in her white-blonde hair drew my eyes and everyone else's.

Speaking of eyes, hers sparkled like grass covered with morning dew. They were the greenest eyes I'd ever seen. Yes, Violet was more a neon sign than a chameleon. I don't know, but maybe even if she'd called herself "Jane Doe," she'd probably have stood out anyway. Some people can't just blend in, can they?

***

As I was saying, her HR paperwork obviously went through, and she'd been working with me for about two years up until recently. Nobody ever came looking for her.

She had been hired with a managerial title but none of the manager duties, and a paycheck two bucks an hour bigger than the rest of us moving stock. She told me up front that it was due to her ability to persuade. Our boss sometimes looked at her funny as he handed her a paycheck, then later exchanged her the cash for it, but he never wavered and was still paying her that money up to her last week.

For Violet's part, since I knew she was picking up extra pay that I wasn't getting, she made it up to me by buying me dinner every Friday... and sometimes lunch on Tuesdays. She was a good friend to me. She said I was to her, too, but I probably already said that.

One day at lunch, she said that her latest boyfriend was pushing her to move into a sales job that had opened up. It wasn't in the warehouse; it was up front. She told me that he was insisting that she would be good at sales, because she was good at talking people into things. He doesn't know how good! I do.

Violet didn't like being pushed. She didn't want to work in sales, she confided, because she feared that she might use her irresistible powers to make people buy things. At heart, she was a kind person. Violet said that her identity was already made up, so changing into a greedy person might happen too easily. It was the only thing she ever told me made her afraid.

When she turned down the job, her pushy boyfriend refused to pick her up from work anymore. She stopped speaking to him; she told me that she didn't even bother to persuade him. Instead, she asked me for rides. I started driving her.

A month later, my friend Violet was gone.

***

The day before Violet died, I saw her in the corner of the warehouse talking to our manager. They didn't see me. Violet's eyes were shining so bright, I got sunspots on my vision just from the glimpse I got. She must have been persuading him real hard. Later when I clocked out, he told me I got a two buck an hour raise! Everyone else in the warehouse got a dollar, which I found out later. Violet was a good person to do that. I've never said a word about mine being more, but then I was her trusted friend.

Anyway, Violet died on that Friday. Her last, pushy boyfriend came in and tried to pick up her check. He looked like hell. He said that Violet had woken up with a high fever. He'd taken her to the hospital early in the morning, and the hospital admitted her right away. Our manager didn't give the boyfriend her check, but he came out and told all of us that Violet was sick.

As my shift ended that afternoon, the boss came out again, and that's when he told us that Violet had died — not from the fever, but from a freak accident at the hospital.

I read about the accident in the paper the next morning. An oxygen tank had exploded, destroying Violet's hospital room with her in it. It horrified me. My friend had gone to such lengths to make a life, and another person's mistake had wiped it all away. The newspaper reported that the nurse attending to Violet's care was questioned by police. She told them she couldn't recall why she'd taken an oxygen tank into the room. Violet hadn't needed any oxygen.

I went to Violet's funeral, which was on the Monday after. It was Stephanie's funeral, too, I guess. Or, was it Jennifer's? I guess it doesn't matter. I think of her as Violet Skye. That's who she was to me.

I paid my condolences to her barely-boyfriend and left the funeral. She hadn't made him forget her before she passed on, and he was grieving hard.

Since then, time has been dragging. I was back in the warehouse Tuesday after the funeral, and work wasn't the same without Violet. The realization of how dull my life was before her arrival increased my grief I think.

***

Payday arrived on the Friday after she died, and for a while I started at my check, with the raise Violet had arranged — or persuaded the boss into. It was a week that felt like it was a month long, as I headed for the credit union.

The line to the teller wasn't as long as usual for a Friday. I made my deposit and left the credit union in record time. Leaving my car parked there, I walked down Hubbard Street. The diner was two blocks down, and I headed straight for it. Fridays were when Violet treated me to dinner. My heart panged and I resolved to treat myself to dinner, grief or no grief, with my pay raise. *Here I come, comfort food*, I thought as I opened the diner door.

Service was better than usual. So was the food. By the time I paid my tab and left the tip on the table, not only did my belly feel wonderfully full, but my heart felt lighter. I left and started walking down Hubbard toward where I'd parked at Hubbard and Main near the bank.

"Excuse me, you forgot your credit card," said a voice behind me.

I stopped, even though I'd used cash, not a card. No one else was on the street, so the voice had to be addressing me. I turned toward the diner, and a server waved at me from the door. "I didn't use a card. Not mine," I said.

She approached me anyway. "Oh, I'm sorry," the server said. She stood in front of me, as if waiting for something.

"Okay, then." I turned to walk away and my foot stopped in mid-air. The woman was touching her eyeball! That's strange enough and rare enough it shocked me to stillness. I watched as she slid her contact lens to the side, and a bright green eye peeked from beneath the brown lens. The greenest eyes I'd ever seen, and I was looking into them again!

"Violet!" I got so happy. I couldn't believe that I had sat eating my dinner in the diner and hadn't recognized her. That's saying something, because she and I'd worked side-by-side for two years.

Seeing the eye, the color of grass, I knew it was her. Beyond that, her hair was dark, flecked with gray; no more white-blonde hair with a purple streak. Her build ran straight up and down, likely due to strategically placed padding beneath her diner uniform, beneath the name tag proclaiming her as "Debra Brown." She didn't look like Violet at all, except for that green eye peeking out.

In a voice *not* the one I was used to hearing from her mouth, she said, "You were a friend to me. You deserve to know I'm okay. I'm gonna go ahead and tell you something, and you must obey. You know what I'm talking about." She breathed in deep, and her exposed eye bored into mine so far I thought she could see behind me. "You'll never tell anyone I'm alive. You won't ever come back to the diner or look for me."

As a single tear slipped from my eye, the newly-named Debra Brown slid the brown contact into place again and said, "Calm yourself for a moment, my friend. Go home and make your life what you want it to be." Then, she walked back inside to her job at the diner.

When I could move again, I walked to my car and drove straight home.

I know Violet's gone from my life, just as if she had died. Since I'm never going to that diner again, I know I won't see her anymore. I still grieve. I wish she'd just made me forget her; that would have been best.

I wish I could persuade people like she did. I would have persuaded my friend to stay. Then, I wouldn't be so lonely now.

A Trick of the Light

The power flickered and went out. The snuffing of the light from the room caused Olive's heart to jump in her chest. It wasn't often that a storm knocked out the power. The hairs on the back of her neck stood up, and her hands began to sweat. She hated the dark.

She blinked repeatedly; it was an automatic response and didn't change her situation. Her eyes slowly adjusted to the darkness, picking up little.

Not only was it late, but with the storm-darkened sky only lightening flashes lit the living room around her. Lightening flashed and she peered around as much as she could in that split-second's worth of light.

No electricity meant no air conditioning, no ceiling fan. With the house closed up, there was no breeze. She started to perspire in the still air. The prickling of fear increased — as it had for humans-in-darkness going back to the beginning of time.

Olive shook her head and attempted to push the fear aside. *It's just a storm. The power will be on soon. I was safely locked in the house when the lights were on, and that hasn't changed.*

Her cell phone binged with a text message and a small spray of light appeared on the table in front of her. She picked up the phone and squinted to read the text message, her eyes blinking a little at the glow. It was from the power company, telling her that there was an outage. *Duh*, she thought.

The phone binged again, and a second message continued with the announcement that the estimated restoration time was three hours from now. Olive resigned herself to the darkness she'd need to live with for the coming hours. *Might as well settle in*, she thought. She pulled her cardigan tightly around her, letting her long hair cover her neck in an itchy yet warming way. Her lips pouted, unseen, as her eyes, on the verge of tears, peered at the now-encroaching shadows. The space she took up on the couch cushion felt smaller and smaller, darkness squeezing all around her.

Unsettled, she rose from the couch and inched forward through the darkness. Her first stop was the laundry room for a flashlight. She shuffled back to the living room, set the flashlight down on the table, and shuffled half-way to the kitchen before realizing that she should be *using* the light. She smacked herself on the forehead, feeling stupid.

Slowly returning to the living room, she felt around until her fingers bumped into the flashlight. She gripped it, fumbled to switch it on, and — more quickly this time — made her way to the kitchen.

Shining the light into the cabinet under the sink, she spotted the emergency candles. Juggling the light, candles, and candle holders, she set each item down on the kitchen counter.

With the matches in her pocket — always there for lighting smokes — she lit the candles and placed them around the house: one in the kitchen, another in the living room, and one in each of the two bathrooms.

Returning to the living room by candle and flashlight — plus a few lightening flashes — Olive sat down on the couch, snug with her back against the couch arm, the wall behind her.

Switching off the flashlight, she tossed it onto the living room couch so it would be close-at-hand if needed again.

She picked up her cell phone. Luckily, the phone had been charging; she knew she would have enough battery for a long while. As an afterthought, she turned down the phone's brightness to further conserve power. At least she could use it during the power outage. The glow from its screen pushed back the dark a little, too.

She scanned the weather reports, which showed that the storm was moving slowly across the area. Reading the same weather predictions on every local news website, she moved on to Facebook. She got bored quickly, then moved on to playing games — avoiding looking at the time display. Time was dragging on enough without her watching it tick by at a snail's pace.

Exactly an hour after the storm had begun, the rain — which had been slowing — stopped completely. No more lightening left her in the midst of shadows. It was not utter darkness, thankfully, with the candles flickering. Around their stuttering patches of light, shadows wavered and crept.

She sat still, listening. Aside from dripping noises outside, the remnants of rain leaving the roof, she heard the creaking of the house, and thunder in the distance.

Not knowing what else to do, she looked around the room, down the hallway, into the kitchen. She didn't look too hard, afraid she might see something looking back. This was her nerves, she knew, and an illogical thought. After a time, she relaxed, becoming more accustomed to the patterns of shimmering light. Her eyelids grew heavy.

Then, a light flickered in the kitchen. It didn't fit the pattern of flickers that she'd been hazily observing. The flame appeared to have grown in brightness.

Olive stood and walked tentatively toward the kitchen, staring at the strangely behaving candle. As she reached it, the candle's flame puffed and almost went out. She jumped back.

The flame danced briefly before returning to its normal flickering. *My breathing must have disturbed it*, she thought. She slowed her breath, turned her head to breathe away from it, and watched the candle suspiciously in side-eye.

Twice more the candle puffed, almost went out, and returned to normal. She exhaled a gust toward it, more from curiosity than a wish to blow it out. The flame didn't move, and the hairs on her neck stood tall. Goosebumps covered her arms.

More than she felt afraid, though, she was puzzled. She backed out of the room and returned to the couch. She sat down and leaned back against the cushion, the wall at her back and the kitchen in her sights. This time, she didn't relax. Her eyes scanned the living room around her, then returned to the kitchen candle. The prickle of fear continued on her neck.

Moving slowly, Olive picked up the flashlight, switched it on, and started pointing it at shadows, sending them fleeing. The next few minutes she wielded the flashlight like a sword in all directions, ending with it pointing into the kitchen.

She felt fingers on her side and quickly put her hand on her ribs, covering the spot where she had felt like she'd been touched. Nothing there, of course. She was home alone. She rubbed the spot with her palm trying to wipe away that sensation. *Probably my t-shirt just twisted, and it put pressure on my side*, she told herself, grasping at logic as her palms began to sweat. She wiped them against her shirt.

The light in the kitchen grew momentarily bright again, then grew much brighter. Shadows disappeared from around the cupboards and counter corners. She stood up without thinking and stared into the kitchen, flashlight aimed into the bright room, its beam lost.

She saw movement, then the candle faded to its normal little flicker, then went out. She swung the flashlight and stabbed its beam into the kitchen. Oddly, she realized she was simultaneously making a mental note to buy more emergency candles. That was no help now!

She felt something brush against her side again. "Damn it," she said aloud as she covered her side with her hand and rubbed away the touch again. She heard the tremor in her own voice and repeated more firmly, "Damn it!"

Olive's flashlight dimmed, then went out. She slapped it against the palm of her hand a few times, as if trying to jiggle more light out of it. No luck. She tried to remember if she had more batteries of the right size, and where they might be.

All the house lights suddenly flashed on. The refrigerator and other appliances beeped. The power was on! She silently thanked the power crews for banishing the darkness.

As she sighed in relief, she grasped that there was a figure standing in the kitchen. The semi-clear form of a man stood facing her, just a few steps away. Her heart leapt.

Then, like smoke in the wind, the figure drifted apart. She watched in horror as its pieces disappeared, one after another, into the tiny bits of shadow remaining in the room's corners. There was only the bright light of the kitchen where it — whatever it was — had been.

How long it had been hiding in the corners, she didn't want to know. She made a note to buy a generator, to never let the darkness spread through the house again.

From that night on, Olive left every house light on, inside and out, all day and night. She didn't want the corners' occupant coming for her in the dark.

The Corrupted Ones

"Her daughter got this necklace for Bobbie," the cashier said as she packed Kate Bly's items into plastic shopping bags. For a moment, Kate thought she must have misheard over the rustling of the plastic.

"I'm sorry, what?" She watched the cashier, Bobbie, closely but the woman didn't respond.

Then Bobbie held the two bags in the air for Kate to take. "Thank you for shopping here at the Dollar Savings Store, Miss Bly."

"Thank you." Kate hustled from the store, unsure what had just happened. After she'd complemented Bobbie's necklace — as a frequent shopper she knew the cashier well enough to make polite conversation — the woman's response, referring to herself in the third person, was a surprise. That wasn't a style of speaking that Kate heard often.

In fact, she'd met a very few people across her 48-year life whom she'd heard referring to themselves by their first names! She'd never noticed it from Bobbie before, and although it was a minor thing, it troubled her.

Making the quick drive home, she tossed the bags on the counter and promptly forgot about the odd conversation.

***

Kate wouldn't have remembered it later, except that she called her sister Monica that evening, hoping to talk about the upcoming holiday and planned family dinner on Thursday. Her sister's response was, "Her husband says he and Monica won't be going to the dinner."

"What?" Kate couldn't believe her ears. "Why are you talking about yourself by name? Since when do you refer to yourself in the third person, sis?"

"You're silly," Monica responded, and ended the call.

Kate stared at the cell phone in her hand. "What the hell just happened?" she said aloud to the empty house.

***

Eating dinner that evening, Kate found herself perusing old memories of a girl she'd known in high school. The girl — young woman, really — stood out in school because she referred to herself by her first name, never as "I." Oddly, Kate could not for the life of her remember what that first name was, despite her classmate's having said it so frequently.

That was one of only a few times that Kate could recall someone in real life referring to themselves in that way. Sure, on TV some of the more annoying characters did so, followed by canned audience laughter at their ridiculousness. Yet twice *today* she'd heard it used, including from her own sister — who was not prone to speaking that way.

With a roll of her eyes, Kate finished her dinner and put it out of her mind with a, "Whatever."

***

The next morning, a Tuesday and two days before the family turkey dinner, Kate was in the middle of making herself a lunch of chicken Alfredo when she realized she was out of cream. She considered using milk, then realized that was gone, too. *I'll make a quick run to the store*, she thought, as she turned off the burner under the chicken and lidded the skillet.

She began driving toward the Dollar Savings Store, then re-routed to the big grocery near downtown. It was an extra ten minutes of driving, but she didn't want to see Bobbie again. Concern flooded her head as she thought of her sister's odd behavior.

She pushed it away as she turned into the store parking lot and parked. *First things first*, she thought. *I can worry about my sister later. I'll just get what I need to finish making my lunch.*

Grabbing milk and cream inside the store, Kate hurried past the other shoppers. Her stomach was rumbling, and the chicken was waiting; she kept her head down as she fast-walked through the aisles. While she didn't know any of the other shoppers, she noted that no one used the word *I* as she passed. All were speaking in names, giving her the creepy impression that they were referring to themselves in the third person as her sister and Bobbie had done. She checked out without exchanging a word with the cashier.

As she reached her car in the parking lot, her cell phone rang. It was one of her parents calling from their shared cell phone. Rolly and Amanda Bly were nothing if not frugal. Answering the call, she heard her mother ask, "Kate, could you bring a salad on Thursday? I don't think I'll have time to make one with the turkey, potatoes, and all. Nothing fancy, though!" There was noise in the background, then, "Oh, and your Dad says to tell you hello. We can't wait to see you!"

Kate responded in kind, promised to bring a simple salad, and ended the call. Not eager to return to the store, but not wanting to disappoint her parents, she dropped her shopping bag in the car and went back into the store to buy salad ingredients. She thought of calling her mother back to ask about Monica, but decided to wait until after lunch.

This time as she checked out, the cashier made conversation. "How are you today?" he asked pleasantly as he scanned the shredded lettuce, tomatoes, croutons, and dressing.

When she answered with one word, *fine*, he followed it up with, "John is having a good day."

Kate nodded as her eyes fixed upon his name tag. Clearing her throat after a protracted silence, she said, "Good for you, John."

She noticed that, across John's name tag hung a necklace that reminded Kate of the one Bobbie wore. She thought about Bobbie, and about the daughter Bobbie said had given her the necklace.

As John turned to tear her receipt from the register tape, Kate saw the back of his neck and gasped in horror. What she'd thought was a necklace disappeared under his skin at the nape of his neck. Two short deely-boppers protruded, wiggling slowly on either side of his spine. They appeared to be made of the same, shiny material as the circle extending around his neck and under his skin. It was not a silver necklace as she'd thought, but something living, and she didn't want to think about what it might be.

He grinned as she ignored the receipt in his hand and grabbed the shopping bag of salad fixings. She ran to her car, locked the doors, and drove home far too quickly.

At home, she locked every door and window, drew the blinds, and turned on the television. The volume she turned all the way up, to blot out any thinking.

Tossing the salad bag in the refrigerator, she continued making her chicken Alfredo. The cream spilled onto the stove, as her hands were shaking.

***

Kate sat on the couch with her dinner plate. As she forked a bite of chicken, her eyes drifted to the television, which she prayed would distract her.

Her mouth went dry. The news anchors shown were both wearing — or rather, had protruding from them — the necklace-like loopy things. She felt her heart thump as it skipped a beat.

The camera angle switched to the meteorologist, who appeared to be leaning as far away from the anchor desk as she could while staying on camera. Her eyes were big as saucers. When one of the anchors turned to look at her, Kate could have sworn the meteorologist trembled — before pointing at a cloud symbol and saying there would be sunny weather tomorrow.

When the station broke to commercial, Kate wolfed her dinner without tasting it, her own eyes wide. She ate without thinking, letting the blaring TV commercials roll through her mind. She didn't want to think about what she'd just seen. She also had a funny feeling that she'd be needing her strength and forced herself to eat every bite.

When the TV news returned after many minutes of commercials, the meteorologist was wearing a necklace and smiling broadly. She mentioned the upcoming holiday, referring to herself by first name, and Kate dropped her plate.

***

Kate changed channels until she found one where the news anchors appeared normal. They weren't wearing the strange things around their necks and spoke normally. She chewed at her nails as she watched the national broadcast. At the end of the hour, in the final minute of the news, mention was made of an odd change in speech patterns on "other" news channels, newspapers, and recent YouTube videos.

Kate leaned forward, listening, her thumbnail clenched between her teeth. The anchor called it a "new trend" as another joked about its quick adoption. One man on-screen questioned how much more odd future trends might get.

Kate blew out a breath, relaxing. She turned off the TV and picked up her cell phone. Everything made sense if this was just a trend that people were emulating.

She wanted to talk with her Mom. She wanted to ask her parents if Monica had started a YouTube channel recently. As unlikely as it was, that would explain everything.

Except the necklaces, she thought. Gooseflesh crawled up her arms, and the little hairs stood up on the back of her neck, as she made the call.

When Kate asked about how Monica seemed, her mother said, "Yes, I thought she sounded odd. But we just saw the news and apparently, it's a new trend. I don't see what's trendy about sounding like a loon."

Kate laughed at that. "It's weird, for sure. I've heard at least two other people referring to themselves by their first name this week. Ugh, I hope it's a trend that passes fast!"

"Me too, Katie. Me too." Her mother paused. "She and her husband aren't coming for dinner," Amanda Bly pouted.

"I know, Mom. It's too bad."

"You're still coming for dinner, aren't you?"

Kate heard the pleading in her mother's voice. "I'll be there, Mom. Don't worry." Gripping her phone tightly, she asked, "Mom, have you seen these weird necklaces people are wearing? Is that a trend, too? The news didn't mention it."

"What are you talking about, Kate?"

She pressed on. "I saw people wearing these necklaces that go under their skin on the back of their necks. With... these... protruding things."

"That's disgusting," her mother said. "You mean like a body piercing but around the neck? I hope I don't see that!"

Kate smiled, recalling how her parents had refused to let her pierce her ears until she was eighteen. It soothed her to think of the cashier at the grocery store, John, as just a man with a body piercing. "Never mind, Mom. I'll see you Thursday. Call if you need me to bring anything else. I have the salad stuff."

***

On Wednesday, the day before the family dinner, Kate sat at the window looking out through the blinds. Her neighbors seemed to be leaving for work as usual. She wondered if any of them were caught up in the new third-person speaking trend and rolled her eyes. She was thankful she couldn't hear them through the window. None whom she saw climbing into their cars appeared to be wearing the neck *piercing* — which she'd decided was what they were.

She turned on the normal, no-neck-loops news station and sat on the couch. Opening the Twitter app on her phone, she saw the *Trending* topics and gasped. Many of the popular hashtags contained *necklace*, *loops*, *speech*, or *illeism*. Not knowing the last word's meaning, she looked it up online, and learned that *illeism* was what she'd heard from Bobbie and her sister: the third-person thing.

Kate began clicking on each trending word to see related tweets — unsure if she felt better or worst that others were intrigued by the phenomena.

***

When she closed the Twitter app hours later, it was near midnight, and she had switched from curious to utterly terrified. From the tweets she'd read, people were scared. It wasn't just the conspiracy theorists or influencers who were tweeting about the illeism and embedded necklaces; some news accounts with hundreds of thousands of followers were tweeting furiously about both, and had been since Monday.

Most tweets were fearful. It was clear that what was happening was *not* a new social trend. Those with the necklaces were seen as sinister, not trendy. Kate had read many tweets by people afraid of family members who were adorned in the "piercing things" or had "spine boppers" along with the change in speech.

None of what she'd read offered a reasonable explanation; nor did she come across any official accounts — government or nonprofit — that were asking for tips or offering help. She'd scanned for hours and had no answers.

She bit her pinky nail, thinking of what might cause a person to change their way of speaking. If a human referred to themselves by name, as if the body was a separate being, then what the hell was actually inside the mind? Monica's speech had changed. *What if it isn't my sister speaking? What if it's evidence of a thing inside her body? A symbiotic or invasive thing?* Goosebumps rose on her forearms. For better or worse, that was one of the more widespread idea that had been proposed in tweets that she'd read.

She was reminded of a movie she'd seen years ago, in the bowels of some streaming service, called *Invasion of the Body Snatchers*. In fact, she believed that she'd seen two different movies with that name over the course of her life. The people in the movies had different personalities after their bodies were replaced by alien copies.

Sure, she'd heard people speaking oddly, but the neck things couldn't be easily dismissed. She shuddered again.

Kate gripped her phone in both hands. She didn't want to read anymore and set it aside.

She didn't sleep.

***

Thursday morning, Kate lay staring at the ceiling. She tried telling herself that the prudent thing to do was to stay home. Skip the family dinner. Stay inside with the doors locked and avoid other people. She could say she was sick. Mom and Dad would understand, maybe. Recalling her conversation with her sister, Kate was glad that Monica wasn't going to dinner. Maybe her parents would be safest having dinner by themselves. *Or maybe, I need to pack up, go get Mom and Dad, and drive far, far away.*

Two days ago, Kate would have found the thought ridiculous. The Kate who had scrolled Twitter for hours knew it to be logical; she should be afraid. A lot of people were afraid.

But take Mom and Dad where? In which direction?

With little to go on, and the news stations compromised — every TV anchor wore neck loops now — there was no way of knowing where to go to avoid this... trending... invading thing. She didn't want to know what the loopy, creepy things were. She did wish she knew what caused it. Was it spread from person to person? Could she have caught it from her trip to the store? Kate shuddered.

No one on Twitter had given any answers; or at least, not answers that gave her comfort. She knew that she didn't want to end up with some weird thing burrowed into the back of the neck, something other than herself talking with her mouth.

Nor did she want to start speaking in the third person, which she now assumed was not just annoying, but likely a side effect of something much, much worse.

If she stayed home... if she was careful... maybe she could avoid becoming one of these corrupted ones. She needed to keep her body from being snatched. For what purpose, she couldn't guess. The people with the necklaces and deely-boppers were still doing their jobs as if nothing had changed. Regardless, that wasn't a life she wanted for herself, nor for her parents. For her sister, she reasoned, it was probably too late.

She said aloud, "I'm going to go get Mom and Dad now. I need to keep them safe from whatever this is." When she didn't refer to herself as Kate, she breathed a sigh of relief. Unconsciously, her hand went to her neck, as she suddenly feared a neck loop might sprout from it.

She called her parents' cell number. "Mom, I'll be there in an hour, okay? I'm coming early to talk to you two."

"That's good. Dad and Amanda will be happy to see you soon."

Kate dropped the phone.

About The Author

K. F. Whatley began her author's journey writing nonfiction desktop publishing books. She moving on to news reporting in 2011, then dove into fiction — picking up where her teen self had left off.

After publishing short items in local literary journals, her first novel, *Making Corrections*, was published in 2018, followed by its sequel, *Triad of Time*, released in 2020.

Based in Eastern North Carolina, with ocean in one direction and foothills in the other, Whatley fills her time with family, gardening, and trying not to trip over house cats.

www.ingramcontent.com/pod-product-compliance
Lightning Source LLC
LaVergne TN
LVHW011716060526
838200LV00051B/2915